I0838535

Published by: Cinnabar Moth Publishing LLC
Santa Fe, New Mexico

Cover Design by: Vanessa Mendozzi

ISBN-13: 978-1-953971-24-1
Library of Congress Control Number: 2021946751

From the Lighthouse

CHAD MUSICK

Chapter One

When he's in a talkative mood, Bigman claims he plucked me from the shore. He was out fishing and saw me float by in a basket of reeds. Scooped me right up to love, and love, and love.

Another scooped-up baby grew up and split the sea right open and walked away, calm as could be. I saw it once in a movie. Bigman tells me it's just a silly story, but there are days I feel like I too could split the ocean open. Maybe silly stories can still be true stories.

If I could split the ocean, I'd walk away and never come back. If he was being nice when I left, I'd take Bigman with me, but he'd have to follow my rules. Rule number one, he'd have to let me call him John. Everyone else calls him that, but he reminds me every day. *I'm Bigman*, he'll say, *and you're Knot*. Sometimes he even says it out loud.

He's been quiet all morning, Bigman has, quiet enough that he doesn't even mutter at me why it is he's not talking. But I know.

It was a dark and stormy night, but it wasn't supposed to be. I heard him myself when he promised the neighbors a fine, clear evening. *Have a great wedding party! Have cakes and drinks and fireworks and open presents.*

The way he said it, he wasn't telling just them. He was also taunting me.

Please, lemme go. The minute he said no, I regretted having begged. He owes me for that.

Since the mess with the old neighbors, I have to beg if I want to see people. Nobody likes me anymore, even though I'm the same as always.

A long time ago, there'd been the neighbor girl, Annea. Has there ever been a more perfect name? She hadn't cared I was strange. As far back as then, the grounds outside our lighthouse were dying. The trees were leafless through the whole year, and the ground always stank of rot. When the sun crossed the sky, mushrooms would rush up from the ground everywhere shade touched.

But Annea would cross the yard like it was a lush garden and ring the doorbell. Back then the doorbell worked. I don't know whether it does anymore.

Can Knot come out and play? That had been her, ten years old, asking for me, probably also ten or maybe a thousand years old. She didn't care that everyone else thought I looked five. Maybe a tiny six. She knew I was older.

But that had been years ago. She grew up and fell in love and got sad and went away. And I didn't. Didn't grow up. Didn't fall in love. Didn't go away.

I'm still here. It's why it's just me and Bigman, Bigman and me, forever and ever. So *please lemme go to the party?* I would have had such fun.

Get in your room and stay there. That was Bigman, telling me who was boss.

Usually, after Bigman promises nice weather to someone, he's careful to be nice. He lets me stay up late and watch movies, even the ones he's seen a hundred times, and he fries up oodles of fish. The oilier the better.

But I'd forgotten myself a few days ago and run off. I'm not supposed to leave, ever. He reminds me by making his hands louder than his voice. As though I could forget that I'm a prisoner.

Leaving isn't safe. Leaving is against the rules. *Rules are important. A boat without rules will sink off the shore*, he'll say, and a little Knot like me without rules would come undone.

Then what would I be? At best, lost and hungry. At worst, someone might snap me up and love me. I couldn't take any more love without coming apart at the edges.

Bigman doesn't like it when I leave. You know that, though, don't you? Bigman says you're just a birth mark, that I'm talking to myself when I talk to you.

Take your face out of your hand.

We've learned to hide it, you and I.

You're a blot a blight a bite a flower of ugly in a field of hideous. But I know you're special. You're the only one that's been with me all these years, yeah? My parents threw me away before I even knew them. Annea ran away when she grew up, and I haven't yet. I'm probably eighteen, or maybe twenty or eighty. It can be hard to remember. So you ought to be old, too. But you're still small like me. Everyone still thinks you're a nothing.

After Bigman denied me the party, left me to be alone so he could rally his allies on the computer and storm some imaginary cave, I could hear the sounds of the fun from south of our tower. The music drifted over the waves and broke free of the mangrove tentacles and finally crept up the walls and into the window of my room.

I huddled down in my blankets, stuffed up my ears with my pillows and my clothes and my fingers and still it pounded at me.

We're having fun, it taunted me. *And you're not.*

I went to the window and screamed at them, and their fun stopped being so fun. The moon grew dimmer when clouds scudded in from far away on the ocean. A storm aimed itself like *disappointment* right at the party, at the fireworks that were just starting.

Fweeee! There goes a firework, spiraling into the sky.

Boom. And the lightning strikes it.

And then? It was a dark and stormy night, oh yes oh yes. The pyromancer must have set the fireworks to go off in sequence. The lightning shot down a dozen before anyone realized it wasn't part of the show. The thunder drowned out the hateful music.

And the rain, oh the rain! Bigman says wedding cake is sweet, that it's like eating a little slice of sugary heaven. But my sickness means I can't ever taste it.

Not even a little bite.

It's a magic sickness, he says, because I saw a show about diabetes and they could eat sugar sometimes. Sometimes they even had to. *It's a magic sickness, not diabetes. And stop watching those shows.*

I think I remember sweetness. Before the trees died, I must have pilfered fresh oranges from the grove. Sweetness was the taste of juice escaping down my chin, mingling with the delicious knowledge I have now, that Bigman had lost track of me for a moment. Maybe forever! That last is my foolishness. Bigman would never lose me forever.

He loves me too much for that.

I bet cake doesn't taste so good after the rain has come down on it. The burning embers of the aborted fireworks came down like broken promises, and the rain fell harder and harder, first washing off the frosting and then cratering the spongy deliciousness of the cake.

The little statue of the bride and groom fell over, toppled to the table, tumbled to the ground and was smushed underfoot by the fleeing people.

That's what I think, anyway, because I don't see so well when I'm being the storm.

If it didn't happen that way, Bigman wouldn't be in such a foul mood.

#

My window is the world, high above itself. The afternoon showers have finished, and I can hear the peacocks croaking murderous lies to each other somewhere far south. Nothing but mushrooms lives here anymore, not since Bigman stopped taking care of things. There must have been a time when he took care, but I don't remember it.

Once, he told me, *this was meant to be a lighthouse. Your room was supposed to hold a giant lamp to warn the ships from the shore.* My room doesn't warn ships, though. Without the lamp, I live in a useless tower with a beautiful view. On a clear day, I could probably see all the way to happiness, if my sight were better and I took off my goggles.

In the story, Rapunzel let down her long golden hair and her prince climbed up it and rescued her. If a prince comes for me, he'll have to use the stairs. Once, I told Bigman that.

Let me tell you how the world works, said he.

No prince will come. My hair is not long. My hair is not golden. It is short and thick and spiked, the white of fish bones, more porcupine quills than beauty.

Lucky I don't need rescuing.

Sneaky as a strangler fig, I put on my explorer dress, check my goggles, climb out the window and edge down the tower to the library window. The tide is going out, releasing the smell of algae baking under the sun. Fishing will be good, when we go.

In the library, Bigman sits at his computer, looking out the other window. He doesn't notice me slipping in, doesn't hear the step of my feet on the timbered floor. Bigman thinks he's the only one with secrets, but I've learned to keep some, too. *Don't see me, don't hear me*, I tell him.

Here he is in front of me, rubbing his wounded thighs with one hand while he types with the other. Without looking, he wipes his bloody hand on the towel he keeps by the desk.

Even sitting down, he's taller than I am. As though I could forget, he'll remind me. *You'll never be big like me*, he says. I'm small, and I stay small, and so he is the one who forgets. You learn a thing or two over the years, you do.

When he's hurting most, he reminds me he plucked me from the shore, and took me home to love, and love, and love, and I bit him for his troubles. I wish I could remember the taste of it.

That bite still bleeds, he tells me sometimes.

Whenever he says it, I grin at him, showing him the same pointed teeth that pierced him.

Most times when I peek in on the library, he's playing video games. He rages when his knight falls, screams in victory when he wins, yells at the people in his headset to learn how to play. He throws things a lot. I like to watch him lose.

Today, though, he's emailing.

Re: Last night's weather

I know you're upset about the storm, but nobody could have predicted it. I only promise to make my best efforts, not a miracle. You can keep the other half of the payment, and I'll keep the deposit. Deal?

No thanks to Bigman that I can read. He kept me from school, and I learned to stop begging. He thinks I watch only cartoons, but I've learned more than he knows from my shows. Even the ones I can't remember.

Bigman likes to make deals. He didn't make a deal with me about the storm last night, though, did he? No, he didn't. It's his fault things didn't go the way he wanted.

Back out the window I go, and down the tower and down the beach to the water. I'll have plenty of time to return before Bigman realizes I'm not in my room. He won't need to hunt me down because he won't know I was gone.

The blue crabs are playing in the surf, and I chase the seabirds away from them. Our beach used to be popular. Children would drag their parents here, and the families would pick along the shore to find discarded shells. The children would scare off the birds and giggle at the sand between their toes.

A few people still come. The ones who don't know.

The locals stay away.

Away from the shore, back at the house, the afternoon heat is baking the rot that used to be an orchard.

The mangrove trees, brought by wind or chance, have taken root along the shore, and it won't be too many years before they've eaten the beach entirely.

Bigman has never liked the mangroves. *They're not supposed to grow this way*, he'll say. He's tried burning them a few times. Tried poisoning them. Tried cutting them. Nothing gets rid of them.

He doesn't like things that don't grow like they're supposed to. That means me, too. I know it, and I lie among the mangrove roots and let the waves lap at me until I'm calm, and then I go home, climb my tower, and pad downstairs on salt-wet feet.

Bigman is playing video games now, and I let him see me.

Bigman with a big nose, and it's useless. I could smell the brine and the seaweed and fish scale on me from miles away, and he just wrinkles his nose standing right next to me. He doesn't know it means I was at the water, in the water, of the water.

You always stink, he says. *Go take a shower. Not a bath, a shower.* And I laugh and laugh as I sit in the tub while the shower head fills a bath for me.

#

Let's go fishing, Bigman says when he's decided I'm clean. He must not be too mad about the storm.

It's the evening that we should have had the night before, the sun at our backs as we head down to the brackish water with my fish bag and his pole.

Our shadows are spreading in front of us, and he's Bigman of course, but I'm Bigman, too. *Rawr*, I raise my arms up with my bag, and the shadow me rears up as a serpent, taller even than Bigman. I could snap him up in my jaws, *chomp chomp chomp*.

He doesn't like it when I'm silly, but we're going fishing and so it doesn't matter much. The fish will make us both happy. He never gets tired of catching them.

When we go together, we don't take the secret ways to the secret beach. That means walking through the gardens. Bigman can't walk quickly. He shuffles himself along. He used to be a lot faster, but time has taken a toll on him. Like he got double time and I got none. He says I'm bigger, but I don't feel bigger. I see he's older. Maybe older than me and surely older than he used to be. He is getting smaller every year.

When your beard reaches the ground, will you die?

Maybe he doesn't know. When he plays video games, the kids make fun of him. He's an old man with an old man voice and an old man body, bent over like a dying tree.

Can you hear the beetles in the wood?

He doesn't answer me, but the beetles do.

We can hear ourselves.

The garden is a dead thing if you only look at the outside. Inside, it's not dead, just changing. It's shedding its skin like a hermit crab moving from its shell. Soon it will look for new clothes.

Mushrooms come, the beetles say. They're usually right, but it's been a decade since the last tree died. Maybe they're wrong, this time. Maybe they mean that mushrooms come for Bigman.

When we get to the water, the tide is low but rising. Bigman pretends he's going to use his pole, just in case anyone comes by.

We're alone together, and he sits in the water. He winces when the first salt hits his wounds, but he rubs his legs softly, scoops water onto them and winces again, until he gets used to it.

The pink froth doesn't scare the fish. They're used to blood in the water. It's only people that get funny about such things.

Go ahead and catch us some dinner? He smiles when he asks. It means all of me is forgiven for last night's storm, and he didn't catch me sneaking out earlier.

I leave my clothes like a castoff cocoon on the beach. The evening is peach silk, ballet slippers, and a sleek dress. Maybe tomorrow I'll wear a tuxedo and top hat. Some days, the costumes are all I need.

Them and the sea. In the water, I am home.

Come see what I have in my bag. I call out to the fish, and they come to look. I don't let them back out, except the young ones.

I swim for a while even after the bag is full and writhing. At sunset, the mermaids—*manatees*, the Bigman in my head corrects—drift by to see what I'm doing and whether I've left any trinkets for them.

The day is coming.

Mermaids aren't supposed to talk. They never have before. They like to gather up people's junk, bits of polished glass, whatever is shiny, but they don't talk to me. Maybe I've been swimming too long and have a brain fever. Bigman has warned me about the fevers.

I swim back to the shore and get dressed while Bigman starts creeping back, carrying the bag of fish. Out of the water it's too heavy for me. They still flop around. Lucky us, it means they'll still be twitching when we get back to the house.

Bigman will chop off their heads and tails. We'll feed those to the clowder of cats that live on the fringes of our blight. Blackie is here, which is why I'm telling you about the cats.

Fish tonight, Knot?

Blackie must smell it on me. She likes me best. Some of the other cats are shy, but crooked-tail Blackie has been forward ever since she was a kitten. I give her a toothy grin and she gives it right back.

We walk so slowly back, so slowly that I'm skipping circles around Bigman as he plods along, and Blackie is batting at the bag with her claws pulled in. She doesn't like them getting stuck.

Every year Bigman is getting slower. Maybe soon he'll stop entirely, and I'll leave him here in his empty castle on his ruined lands. See how well he fishes when I'm not here to help.

Did you leave the door open? He looks at me sharpish, and I shake my head in denial.

Of course I didn't.

Sometimes, over the years, the nasty kids from far away have invaded.

"Are you a boy or a girl?" It's the first thing they always demand to know. And Bigman always shoos them away.

That's nobody's business unless you're romancing them, he says each time, and laughs.

Can you even see with those things on? It's the second thing people ask. Bigman doesn't shoo those people. Sometimes he is those people.

That's nobody's business unless I'm hunting them, I say. I don't laugh.

The door is open, and Bigman staggers up the stairs as fast as he can and yells in pain. "They took my computer!"

The vegetables are scattered on the floor, and they've daubed the floor in what looks like blood but smells like ketchup.

The day is coming.

Bigman's good mood is gone, and he leaves it to me to chop the heads off the fish.

#

This bright morning, Bigman swaddles his legs in gauze and shuffles his way to his truck.

Clean up the mess. I'm going to get a new computer.

What if I wanted to go?

But of course I never go. It's been a long time since I left our grounds. At least that Bigman knows about.

Cleaning up is boring. Boring!

Good enough, to pick the fallen things up. Good enough, to splash some water on the floor and wrap my feet in towels and waddle around like Bigman.

I find Blackie and her friends and give them last night's fish heads, and I'm still alone.

If I left, maybe he'd be too slow to catch me?

Better not. It's not about speed, now is it?

What d'you think, Blackie?

Search his treasure? Is that what you think? Oh, you wicked beast. You clever beast.

I can't ignore my friend's suggestion.

Bigman's room is a mess. He'd call me a pig if mine were like this.

Among the dusty cables, the half-read novels, the musty old clothes, there is a bag of silver fragments that click and sparkle.

You know what they are, don't you? They're just like you. I didn't know he'd kept them.

The last time I saw these, a year or a decade ago, it's so hard to remember, he was telling his lady friend that they were guitar picks. He'd even used one to strum a bit, and she'd laughed in delight.

He sent me away when he noticed me, when I forgot to make him ignore me. The woman had looked at me in surprise, too.

She'd been wearing a costume, just like me. All shimmery scales and big poufy hair.

And shame.

Yes, and shame. I could smell it on her. Bigman never smells of it. He sometimes smells of anger or jealousy or pain, but never of shame. He's like a cat, that way.

The fragments beg to be touched. They smell of loneliness, but I don't like to look at my skin.

You say you're white, I asked Bigman, once. *What color does that make me?*

Because Bigman's the white of pig belly, of earthworm. Until he gets sun, and then he's the white of unripe tomato, when it's not green anymore but the red is just bursting to the surface. Too soon to eat, too late to yank from the vine.

You're white too.

The white of maggots.

Or milk. Blackie thinks she's clever.

I fetch some milk and pour for her. Maybe she is clever.

So I'm white, but my hands are red fishnet on white pain, except for you, my friend. You fit in my palm, and Bigman doesn't take you because he can't recognize that you're special, too.

But your friends are back now.

Solve the puzzle.

Bigman showed me jigsaws once, when the weatherman reported a hurricane was headed our way.

Our house should stay dry and safe, shouldn't it? Our neighbors might be in danger, but I'm not, and you're Knot, yeah?

He stayed up all night with me, showing me how to find the edges first, to piece things together by shape and color, by touch and memory. And he was right, that the storm didn't bother us. It had been good it didn't bother us, so we had time for the puzzle.

So I know what to do now, don't I?

I start at the edges, the places on my hands where the red lines stop and give way to the unbroken ugliness of my arms.

The first one is the hardest to find.

And then, I do.

It's a relief when it sticks to me with only a little help, like taking the first swim of the day and feeling my bladder let go.

And then the second, the third, the fourth.

Finally, the last one.

The clicky silvery of the fragments, which Bigman had once used to play a guitar for his friend, feels like part of me now.

My hands are silver gloves. The gloves feel more real than my skin ever did.

And there you are, nestled in the center, almost glowing with happiness that you're not alone anymore.

And I remember so much. I know now what Bigman has stolen, because these are mine and these are stolen. Each of them is a year of my life, and without them I was left with only the shadows. I could remember Annea, and that we must have been friends, but not that we loved each other. Not that we whispered secrets. At least, until the deaths.

And I remember Bigman, and what he's done, and who he is, my captor. Bigman won't like this at all, will he?

I hear his truck wheezing up the road. I've dallied too long in my memories, and I want to blast his truck with lightning, strike him dead and run, but in remembering I know it would do no good. He is a crooked old man only in his body, just as I am a Dragon only in my soul.

Blackie knows none of this, only that I have something new. She goes into my hands.

Such lovely hands.

I put her out the door. *You know Bigman doesn't let you stay.*

One at a time, I pluck off the scales.

That's what they are. That's what you are, my heart.

One gone, and a drop of blood, and I can't hear the dolphins playing in the distance.

Two gone, and more blood, and I can't smell oysters grilling anymore.

Each one plucked is a loss, a diminishing. By the time I pluck the last one, I'm bleeding and crying, and I don't know which is blood and which is tears, and I am so small.

So alone. I can remember something is missing, but not what, like waking up suddenly from a wonderful terrible nightmare hope dream.

I stuff them all back in the bag. All except you. You, I leave. You are mine alone.

The bag of scales, all the blood gone and drunk by the scales, goes back into his closet, and he rattles the door and curses as he drops the first box and goes back for the other.

We don't talk about his computer. We don't talk about the scales.

He is Bigman, and I am Knot. Not yet ready to escape, but hoping that's what the mermaids meant, that the day of my escape is coming.

#

We still have some left from last night.

Bigman doesn't want to go fishing again. Every

time he leaves home, he comes back worse than he left. All afternoon, he tinkers with his new computer. Cursing, sweating, exclaiming with delight as he finally gets it working.

When I make myself small, he doesn't notice me. You know that doesn't mean I can just leave. If he wants me, I have to make myself bigger, show him where I am so that he doesn't come searching.

But now he's distracted. I bring him a whiskey.

I didn't ask you to bring this.

You don't want it? The smell of thirst is pouring off of him already. I start to take it back, and he snatches it from me.

It's not long before he's not thinking of me at all, and I'm out my window and down the tower. But I'm full on fish, and the grounds sound wrong. Water is splashing where it doesn't belong, in the fountain.

The green wizard—*the arborist*, Bigman would say, if he could read my thoughts—said the water was poisonous and that's why all the trees were dying.

When Bigman turned off the water, it just made them die faster. They were never meant for the weather we have, too little rain because it makes Bigman's bones creak and so we sing *rain rain go away*, and it does.

But now I can hear the fountain running, splish splashing against the evening noises. I pick my way along the stiff weeds. Even they don't have enough to keep them alive. The driveway is torn asunder by poisoned tree roots, leaving only a narrow way where Bigman's old truck shambles through on the days he goes out.

That's not many days anymore. The delivery truck brings us vegetables and other groceries once a week, but we mostly eat the fish. I don't mind, but he gets sick of it sometimes.

Hello, fountain. My face looks back up at me in dirty water. My reflection is wearing its own goggles that reflect the fountain. The little stone boy is cheerfully pissing rusted water into the pool.

There's a valve at the base of the fountain. I know the secret, where the water can be turned off. It's no good to waste it. We still need it in the house. It's too poisonous for trees, but Bigman says it's good enough for us.

I'm underwater on this place already. I can't afford to sell it and I can't afford to move. He spends a lot of time worried about money, but not much time trying to find any, it seems to me.

I twist the valve, but the water doesn't change. It keeps leaking into the fountain. Another broken thing that Bigman will say we don't have the money to fix and won't come do it himself.

The sun goes down all of a sudden, while I'm trying to get the water to stop. When I come up to check it, the water isn't just there anymore, it's glowing like so many of the fish do if one is quiet and doesn't threaten them.

A trail of faint light leads off toward the edge of our property, where the trees and the bushes start growing again. I risk catastrophe and lift my goggles, and the light vanishes. I put them back on.

I haven't meant to follow the path, but I find myself now in the dark beyond my home, away from the angry neighbors with their jealous wedding cake.

The old neighbors used to be old, but these ones are young. They don't notice me hiding in the bushes watching them.

The adults don't, anyway. I've been spotted by the child.

You don't see me. She ignores that and sees me anyway. Soon, she's sidled up to the bushes and is staring right at me. When they're that close, it's hard to make them stop noticing.

The day is coming. She whispers it at me. I don't know what she means, even though I feel like I should.

She whispers again. *My birthday is coming. I'll be six. We're going to have a party. You should come.*

Oh, my heart, I have missed the little girl so much since she grew up. What was her name again? This one isn't her, I know that, but she's taller than me, like the other one was, and when her blue eyes look at my blue lenses, the ones that hide my milky eyes (*like damn cataracts,* Bigman says), she doesn't step away and she doesn't reach out to poke them.

Will you come to my party? She's so hopeful, so pure and pretty and just who I wish I could be, that against my better judgment I nod. She smells like kindness. *I'll come to your party.*

I'll be six. Bring me a present.

Her parents call her away. They don't notice me. The way it should be. When the girl waves goodbye to me, they ask her. "Who are you waving at?"

Her voice is smiling. "My new friend. There's a new friend in the bushes."

They cluck at her and laugh.

"No, there's Knot." They know I'm nobody's friend.

Recognized, I dash away home. My heart is hammering loud enough Bigman must hear it rattling the glass of his window as I climb past, but when I'm inside I hear him snoring. He knows nothing.

Chapter Two

Voices floating to my room from downstairs wake me. Sometimes Bigman orders a woman online, but they always show up later in the day, and he always tells me to hide upstairs before they arrive. This is different. Customers.

Today is a day to be unseen, and so I dress as a ninja. Ninjas are best at killing people. If I'm very lucky, it will come to that, and I will need to avenge Bigman's death. For honor, not for love. I probably won't be so fortunate.

Some days I'm not sure whether Bigman should keep on. Maybe he should go like my memories and fade and rot, but the costumes he buys remind me why I don't smother him in his sleep. That, and he would be mad if I did it.

Bigman has his own costumes, and I creep down to the middle floor with its wrap-around walkway that looks down on where he holds court. The people who built this house couldn't make up their minds about what should be here, so there's the tower where I'm held and this hall where I can look down unseen. Three shapes below.

From the voices, it's the big young people who own the little girl. I slip down the stairs and tell them not to see me.

"We want to be sure the party for our little Mary goes well." The woman says it, and the man looks ashamed. He's not a believer, or he's a believer in the wrong kind of thing. Bigman is dressed in his wizard robes today, the long black fuzzy fabric turning his limp into a shuffle. He's spread his cards in front of him and is concentrating, or at least pretending to. He's tried to explain to me how these spells are supposed to work, but it's never made any sense. Might as well pray to the sky.

There's the magician card in the center. It's always in the middle. It took me a few years to figure out how to make it work, and a few more to practice it, though I'll never be good at it. My hands are small, and Bigman doesn't like me touching his cards. Or his dice. Or his anything. *Selfish man.*

The girl isn't here, and so I tell the big people not to see me, and creep close enough to touch. The woman smells of perfume and rotted fruit. Her hair is light brown, the color of dirt where only scraggled weeds will grow.

If you live in the desert, you're supposed to wear white clothes so that the sun will be reflected away and you won't be so hot. I must have seen that in a movie once. The house is warm and humid, and I'm wearing black. But the sun isn't shining straight in, and so I'm all right.

Not the woman.

She's dressed in fabric so thin I can see right through it to her underwear, and so overheated that she's covered with sweat and doesn't even feel when I taste it with the tip of my tongue. *Don't see me don't feel me.* And she doesn't. None of them do.

She's the wrong kind of salty, all sunscreen and misery. Maybe she's new to here, to the whole area and not just to the house. The new ones come the most to Bigman, surprised by the persistence of afternoon rains that bring no relief from the heat.

Her hand swats at her arm where I've just kissed her with my fangs, but I'm long gone, moved on to search through her bag. Useless bits, like most people, and there's the sunscreen, just as I thought.

"The three of swords," Bigman says. The same as it's always the magician, it's always the three of swords. Blah blah blah. "Rain." He shakes his head in mock sadness.

"The four of pentacles." Yes yes, next he'll tell them that they hold onto their money too tightly. But he's got the woman enthralled. Her man is looking around angrily. I can smell his scorn. It's strong enough I know I wouldn't like his taste, so I don't even bother with a nibble.

Bigman is still selling them on giving him money to make the rain go away, both from their party and from their lives. But how can he, when the man is the rain? How does he not see that misfortune follows this man like a hungry turtle? Misfortune follows all fathers that way. I know it's true, but can't remember why.

I go back to the woman's bag. And there, in the bottom, is a handkerchief. It's blue and silver and all the best colors, and most of all it doesn't smell like her. It smells like a child. *Mary.* They said that's her name, didn't they?

She will be my best friend. I know it as certainly as I know when the tide will come in. But for that to become true, I have to go to her party.

Bigman is concentrating, and when I give him a nip on the neck, he just swats at whatever he thinks it was. I'm back upstairs before the first drop of blood even beads up on his skin.

I am the avenging wind.

The avenging wind won't get invited to a party by the ones who count, but a costume change can hide my true nature. I switch into a full princess dress, with a tall pointy hat to hide my hideous mane and long gloves to hide my gruesome claws. When I pull the gloves on, I feel like a betrayer. I know these are not the gloves I should be wearing, even though I think they're my best.

Tromp. Tromp. Tromp. Hear me coming. I'm coming down the stairs.

And they all look up and watch me walk the last few steps. Bigman is mad, I can tell, but he can't get mad enough that they can see it. He knows what I am, but only a few see something other than a child. You can't yell at a child if you want people to give you money.

I was invited to the party, I tell Bigman. He doesn't want to tell them. *I'll hurt you later if you don't say*. I don't like warning him, but sometimes he's reluctant.

"Lucy wants to know if she can come to the party."

So I'm Lucy, am I? All right. I've been Lucy before, and Luke, and maybe I've been Judas or Magdalene, even. The names all blend together.

People raised with good manners don't shrink back at the sight of someone like me. The woman has been raised with the best of manners. She gives me a curtsy without getting up, and waves at me and smiles hard enough I know she thinks I'm mentally slow.

The man, though. He knows a fellow monster when he sees one, even if he doesn't know he's knowing it, and he suddenly finds he needs to leave the room. "Important phone call," he tells Bigman. I'm sure.

"Of course Lucy can come to the party. We'd be delighted to have her there." She talks to Bigman but doesn't make eye contact with me.

Her voice is as brittle as a dried starfish.

We'll discuss this later, Bigman tells me. He still thinks he can talk me out of it.

#

The people have gone, *Mary and Joe*, or so they said, and Bigman is shouting for me. He can wait. Or he can walk up the stairs to my tower. To my cell.

Outside, a kestrel is hovering, staring at me. I open the window for it. *Come in, come in!* It circles the tower once and looks at me again.

The day is coming. Better hunting where there's life. It flies away.

As though I need its advice.

Bigman has started banging the pans in the kitchen. Maybe he's cooking. More likely he's just doing it to hurt me for not coming down when he calls. Do you hear through my ears and hurt through my body at the clangor?

I come downstairs as a sailor. When he's in a good mood, Bigman laughs at this one.

As I suspected, he's not making food at all, just sitting on a chair and banging on the pan with a knife handle. When I let him see me, he puts the pan on the table. He's still holding the knife, but it doesn't seem like he remembers that. It's more habit than intention.

Why are you like that? The money I make keeps us afloat. Do you want us to starve?

There's still some chopped fish in the refrigerator, and I pull a stool over to the stove and start frying them. *Want some?*

He shakes his head irritably. More for me, then. Seems to me he shouldn't complain about starving and then turn down good food. If he weren't so aggressive, I'd laugh at the idea of us starving. Won't happen unless he gets allergic to fish.

Did they give you the money?

Some smacks in the head are friendlier than others. He's not friendly today.

That's not the point.

It is the point. He knows it's the point. I show him my teeth and he sighs and sits down again, out of reach.

Fine, give me some fish.

I don't want to share now. I could throw the hot oil in his face, make his skin mottled like mine, but he might catch me anyway. Better to share and wait for a better time.

I'm going to the party. You heard her invite me.

Bigman sighs, like he's the one suffering. We both know that money isn't going entirely to food. He won't be suffering much, pretty soon. I'll tempt him with the drink myself if he doesn't stop bothering me.

You know it's going to cause trouble. It's a child's party. There will be lots of people there. Children. Maybe even dogs.

He's lying about the last. They didn't smell of dogs, and their yard didn't smell of dogs. Where there's a dog, there's the smell of a dog.

I don't care. I want to go. He thinks I'm scared of dogs, but I'm not. They're just too noisy and too nosy.

And you don't have a present for her.

She could have a costume. I'm tired of the ladybug. Maybe my new best friend would like it. *I need a new one anyway. I want to be a knight, with silver armor.*

He looks at me suspiciously. The fish is ready, and I serve us both. I almost get him with the fork before he snatches it from my hand and slaps me away.

Behave, or I'll lock you away.

As if I would care.

And I'll bar the windows. They're a hazard anyway.

Does he know, or does he only suspect? If this were a spy movie, I could crawl out through the ventilation duct. But the only air in the tower comes through the windows and their leaky frames. No ventilation duct.

Get me a knight's armor.

Bigman denies me. *Too expensive. You can have a tunic.*

This must be the part where I have to earn my knighthood. I should have expected this from him. *You're not the king. You don't decide.*

I'm the king of you.

In the tussle, I knock his food to the ground. He catches me by the hair. I swipe at him and scratch him a good one on the arm. When he sees he's bleeding from his arm and not just from his legs, he drops me.

I'm in rebellion. Down with the king.

He sighs, admitting defeat, and so I fetch the first-aid kit and help him bandage the cut.

It's going to scar, I think.

Bigman wasn't pretty before, and so it doesn't matter much. Let him be ugly like me.

I'm going to that party. If you're worried, help me do it right.

His hair is turning gray, and his skin is starting to sag, and it takes him longer and longer to recover when he crosses me. Do you think he's getting old? He's been the same for so long that I had decided he would never grow old. I know Blackie's mother and grandmother. I even knew the great grandmother, before she died. Bigman is no cat, with a short and fast life.

I will never find Bigman with his spine crushed and his eyes eaten out, the way Blackie's brother went.

I'll help you, but only if you don't leave the house until then.

But we know, don't we, that his words don't really mean anything?

#

When the sun sets, we go fishing again. It's special because Bigman doesn't like to fish in the dark. It's my favorite time.

I know you want something. What?

He spooks a little. *Stop reading my mind.*

I just snort. No need to be a mind reader. The smell of his worry is almost overpowering. How does he even stand it?

You shouldn't go to the girl's party.

I want to. You said I could.

Remember what happened with the last one?

We're at the beach, and I shed my false skin and run down into the water. I hear him calling after me, but he's not going to come in.

It's not fair to bring up the last one. That was different, and not my fault.

Mary's party is tomorrow before lunchtime, and even though he doesn't want me to go, Bigman has wrapped some dolls for her. I hope girls still like dolls. The other one did. The one who grew up. I wish I could still remember her name. I know it was something beautiful.

The night is warm and calm despite a scattering of bright clouds, with barely any waves. I swim so far out, far enough that Bigman calls after me and I ignore him. I dive down deep, and there are the fish, faintly glowing at me. I sing to them, telling them how safe my sack is, and how plentiful its food. Bigman doesn't mind that I lie to the fish. He's only upset when I lie to him.

Good people don't lie. That's what he says, even though he knows I'm neither good nor people. Never will be either.

But tonight, the fish are scared. At first, I can't hear why. Most fish don't say much at all, not even the *glug glug glug* that cartoon fish say. The mermaids and the unicorns and all the other big monsters, even the gentle ones, keep them scared and quiet. But the fish are dashing away in fear, and I hear something coming after them. *Flee or be eaten. Away! Monsters here!*

It takes a while, but I find the source of it. A kraken, though one of the smaller variety that might be the guest of honor on a fancy cooking show.

Why are you chasing them away? They were to be my dinner.

Under the water, the light doesn't make it hard to see, the way it does back on land. I see him just fine, staring unblinking at me, his tentacles slowly undulating.

The day is coming, he says.

What would you know about day, you?

The light comes through, as you well know. It's only the deep ones and the blind ones who can't tell day from night.

Fine, the day is coming. But so is the night, and I'm hungry. Go away and let me catch fish, or I'll make you my dinner.

I swipe at him, but he's too fast for me to catch while I'm holding the bag. He jets away, leaving a cloud of foul ink. But he doesn't go far. Only out of reach.

Listen, clawed one. The day is coming, even if you ignore it.

I know it's coming. I'm going to the party. I even have a present.

You know that's not the day. In your hearts, you know.

I don't like the way the kraken laughs, the mad whirl of arms around him and the wink of a glow as he swims away.

When he's gone, I sing to the fish again, but the stink and the blur of ink is scaring them off. I swim to a new place and sing some fish into my bag before heading back to Bigman.

At the shore, he's waiting impatiently. He huffs at me when I emerge from the water.

Took you long enough. I was about to send the Coast Guard.

Ahh, but he wasn't. We both know that. Time was he could explain me, but I'm too old, too little, too strange for that now. Hard enough when his customers come, but careful costuming can have them see a child instead of a monster.

I leave the bag of fish in the surf for him to fetch out and head back alone, taking the short way home. His slow walk will give me time to wash before he returns.

I'm too agitated for a bath. It would just make me want to go back out to the deep and find that fish-with-airs and make him tell me just what he means. I settle for a quick rinse, and change into slipper-footed rabbit pajamas before Bigman gets back.

Before he does, I've got cartoons on the downstairs TV. If he doesn't like it, he can just watch something else upstairs. A whole episode passes, all twenty-two minutes of fun and eight minutes of advertisements, before he wheezes through the door with only a half bag of fish.

Where'd the rest go? I caught a full bag.

When I get closer, I smell the stink of blood and something foul. His pants are ripped, and his leg is bleeding more than usual.

A dog attacked me, and I had to drop half the fish just to get away. You should have been there.

That's the other stink. I couldn't place it before.

I chop the fish while he washes his leg. No sense in dinner spoiling.

The bite is shallow, though his pants are ruined. I pour hydrogen peroxide in it, and we both watch it bubble up without saying anything.

I'm sorry, I admit. *I'm sorry I didn't listen about the dog. I'm sorry I wasn't there.*

If he thinks this is going to keep me from the party, though, he's wrong. I don't like dogs, but I'm not afraid. They are not the only ones with fangs and claws.

#

When Annea, that's her name, I remember now, comes and knocks on the door. I know I'm dreaming, but this is one of the dreams I like. I can tell it's not real because she's so much smaller than the last time I saw her.

"Can you come over?" She's wearing a summer dress covered with sunflowers. It's one of my favorites.

"Can I go play with Annea?" I call upstairs to Bigman. He's doing something on his computer, but I don't remember what. I didn't pay much attention back then.

"Just come back when you're done."

Annea grabs my hand, and I shut the door behind us as we leave. I'm wearing shorts and leather-strap sandals.

It doesn't take long to get to her room. Even when I was awake, it never did, but now it's fast as a blink.

She opens her closet and we walk in. She shows me her newest treasure. "Dad had this made for me. A seamstress came and measured me for it and everything. She said if I were a grown-up, she'd make a dummy of me so she wouldn't have to measure, but I grow too fast for that."

Annea pulls off her sunflower dress and hangs it up, then takes a new blue one with a white pinafore from a hanger. She puts it on along with a pair of white tights and slips into her favorite pair of black buckle shoes.

"Who am I?" she asks, smiling at me.

"You're Alice," I say. "Too easy."

"Well, I like it. Are going to come trick or treating with me? Dad says he'll drive us into town and go with us."

She knows I can't. I told her last year I can't. Does she say it to be mean?

"I can't have sugar," I remind her.

She blushes and puts her hand on my shoulder. "I'm sorry, I forgot."

"I could still dress up and go with you, maybe? I can ask. I'll promise not to eat any candy. But I don't have a costume."

She grins at me. How many years has it been since she looked at me like that? In my dreams, I never cry, but some mornings I wake up with a damp pillowcase.

Even when she was ten, she was much taller than I am now, so I was never tall enough to reach her shelves, but she grabs a ladder. I help her take down a box of stuff. It's not as heavy as I thought it would be.

Inside the box are clothes she's outgrown. She roots around in it, looking for the thing that feels right. I know now what she's looking for, but I can still remember the excitement I felt then. What treasure would she pull out? She had so many of them.

Finally, after searching for ten hundred hours, she pulls out a furry gray piece of fabric. When she stretches it out, I can see it's a wolf costume.

"For you," she says, "so you have something to wear."

I take off my sandals and pull the costume on over my clothes. The hood makes my ears hot, but it's worth it. The mirror shows that I look very wolfish, ready to eat a Little Red Riding Hood's grandma just to steal her cookies.

Annea is standing behind me, still grinning.

"It's wonderful," I tell her. *You're wonderful.* I don't say that part to her. It would embarrass her, and when this happened I hadn't learned yet that she is the only wonderful person in the world and needed to hear that said.

"Do you have more?" I look up at her, hopeful. "If you have the rabbit, I could be the white rabbit for your Alice."

"Sorry, no." She's really sorry, I can tell.

We play for hours, until the sun has almost set. When her dad calls her to dinner, I take off the costume and hold it out for her.

"You can keep it," she tells me.

I carry my present home with me and show Bigman. He's not impressed, but he never is.

"Can you get me a costume for Halloween?"

He frowns. "You know you can't have any candy. And you have a new costume in your hands."

"I promise I won't eat any. Some places have stickers and things, don't they? And I want to be a rabbit, not a wolf."

"You'll understand when you grow up that being a wolf is better, but I can get you a rabbit. If you eat any of the candy, though, you won't be allowed to go anymore."

"I promise." I mean it. I really do, at least when I say it.

Bigman goes back to his computer, and I go to my room and watch TV. Halloween is coming soon, so there are lots of spooky movies on. If I keep the volume low, Bigman won't know I'm not watching cartoons.

When one of the people in the movie starts screaming like a peacock, I wake. Every morning starts this way, and I hate them.

I wonder what peacock tastes like. Delicious, probably.

#

Today is the day! Today is the day! Beware!

Shut up! I don't shout it back. The peacocks wouldn't hear, and it might wake Bigman. Last night, I made sure he had plenty of fun, plenty of whiskey and games, so that he'll sleep late. I know it's the day, and I know that despite his promise he might try to interfere with me going. He's a liar like that.

I'm giving up one of my treasure chests, just a little one that I can carry, to this party. Not the dolls from him. I'll save those later to give Mary if she needs more presents to be my friend.

Inside the chest, I've put the princess costume that her parents saw me in. I hope she loves it, because it hurts to give it away. I'm keeping the hat. Bigman says the best presents are those we'd want for ourselves. Usually, he's saying that when the present he wants is my silence, but sometimes he's right about things.

Blackie is mewling at the door when I open it, and I bring her some milk.

The sun is ferocious today, perfect weather for Mary's party, just like I knew it would be. Today I've dressed as a genie. I'll be granting Mary's wishes for her birthday, and it lets me wear a veil that hides my goggles.

Today's the day, Knot. Are you ready?

I have everything I need. Are you coming with me? There might be dogs.

She shows me how she can arch her back and hiss and puff herself up to be bigger. *Let them try!*

We head down the path together, me and Blackie. She keeps veering off to check the dry bushes. She emerges from one of them with a dead lizard.

Blackie, don't kill the lizards.

She drops it at my feet. *Wasn't me. Dead already.*

I can smell that now. It's shriveled, like all the

water has been sucked out, but it also smells of smoke. I throw the thing back in the dead shrubs, and Blackie pouts but doesn't leave.

We go to Mary's house, where the party will be, crossing from decay to more hopeful greenery. The smell of dog is stronger now, but its smell doesn't match the kind that attacked Bigman. This is the smell of small and nervous dogs, the kind that whimper and release a submissive puddle when you growl back at them.

You're going the wrong way.

As if Blackie knows the way to the girl's house. I've been there before, and I never get lost going somewhere I've been. I keep going toward Mary's, and Blackie swipes at me, claws sheathed. She knows better than to scratch.

Follow me, Knot. I know the way. Even if she does, so do I. It's not long before we arrive.

A table is set outside, and a dozen presents are set out for Mary, wrapped and ribboned. From inside, I hear the sound of little girls playing. I'm late. I should have checked what time it was to begin, but I was more worried that Bigman was going to stop me.

I put the treasure chest on the table and rap at the door. Mary, the big one, lets me inside.

"Welcome, Lucy!" That's what her words say, but her voice tells me I'm unwelcome. Too bad for her.

A small dog, one of the fat kind with a flat face, comes to see who I am.

You're not wanted, she tells me. *You mean trouble.* She lets out a growl, but she's only pretending bravery.

You'd be a welcome change from fish. I raise my veil and show her my fangs. She slinks away, complaining to big Mary. Big Mary ignores her, the way people usually ignore animals.

None of the other girls are dressed up, but that's all right. It just means Mary probably doesn't already have a princess costume. Somewhere, Blackie stopped following me, and I didn't notice.

I'm glad you came, little Mary whispers to me. *I don't know these kids. They're not my friends.*

I didn't know you could hire girls the way you can hire women. Or if I knew it, I forgot. That's something new to think on for later. Mary takes my hand and leads me into the games. The silk of my glove feels slippery against my palm, and I know she feels it too. She's rubbing her hand in mine to feel it move against her. I made a good choice of gift.

We put a blindfold on you, and spin you around, and then you have to pin the tail on the donkey.

And that's what they do. Sometimes when I'm swimming, a big wave will come and twist me around, and the black surf at night will cut out my vision. But the laughter and chatter of the girls makes it easy to know which way I'm headed.

I stick the tail onto the donkey. When the game is over, I'm the clear winner. The others just stumbled around while everyone laughed. They'd drown in no time at all.

I'd save Mary. Let the monsters of the deep take the others.

Chapter Three

Little Mary takes the paper off each present, one by one, and exclaims over each.

"Thank you for the doll."

"Thank you for the doll."

"Thank you for the doll."

Big Mary takes notes of each present, and Joseph takes video of them being opened.

Good thing I was smarter than Bigman about what little girls like. It would be embarrassing to match everyone else.

When she opens mine, she runs her fingers over the chest before opening it, lingers over the plastic hinges. She pulls the fabric from inside and holds it up against her. Just the right size. Dresses are nice that way.

Thank you.

Little Mary hugs me. So warm. When I was younger, Bigman used to hold me sometimes. Once, I bet he even put me up on his shoulders and walked from tree to tree so I could pull down sweet oranges, even if I couldn't eat them. That must have been before the trees stopped making fruit.

Sometimes Blackie rubs against me, and her fur is warm and soft. Nothing else is warm or soft. *I love it.*

Mary means the gift.

I keep my arms at my sides so she won't stop, but she lets go anyway because Joe is calling out. *Time for cake and ice cream.*

Probably I should leave. Or at least say no. But it's going to be sweetness, redemption after the ruined wedding where Bigman kept me from the cake.

The frosting is in my mouth before I even decide to make a decision. Smelling me eat it, the dog comes back. She's staring at me but not saying anything. *Go away,* I warn her.

And oh, the ice cream. It doesn't have much smell, but the taste is chilly bliss. Why have I let Bigman keep me from this all these years? He's just been jealous, talking his nonsense of a magic disease. If there is any magic in the world, it is ice cream.

Today is the day, the dog tells me. *And now you're not going to be ready.* She runs away in fear, and I haven't even said anything to threaten her. Coward.

The air smells of rot, even though the wind is not blowing from our land. The wind is not blowing anywhere but here, I see.

No hurricane was predicted, but the smell of it

is strong enough that the girls must notice, too. They pretend they don't.

Come play hide and seek. Little Mary grabs my hand and leads me into the house. Can't she hear the windows rattling? The keening of the dogs, both hers and those down the road? Even the peacocks are croaking in fear, not mockery. The whole world is screaming, except the stupid girls and the stupid adults and my friend Mary.

You're It! the girls scream at me. The old and hurtful taunt. They run, and I pretend to count, tell them not to see me anymore.

When I can't hear them running anymore, I go to Mary. Even if I hadn't heard the path of her steps, she is easy to locate from her smell. This is supposed to be a game?

Even though I'm telling her not to see me, she does, just like before, and she runs away.

People don't like to be snapped up, but she's in danger. They're all in danger, but I can only save one of them. I snap her up, grab her hand and make her run outside with me, across her lawn, and back toward home.

We shouldn't go so far, she complains.

Trust me. I have another present for you. I hate to lie to her, but I don't have time to explain. I can hear the TV her parents are watching, and the other girls are hiding, so nobody sees us going.

Blackie yowls at me. *I told you it was the wrong direction.*

Then tell me where to go. I was going to take her back home.

You should leave her. But I don't let go, and Blackie bounds away. We follow her scent. The smell of rot is still following, the wind still circling me. It's moving, chasing me.

Mary runs, but she's painfully slow.

I have another present for you. Something special. I keep telling her so she'll follow. I'll figure out something to give her, some present to satisfy her. The dolls, I suppose. She wouldn't understand the gift I'm really giving her. *Life.* I know how ungrateful girls, even the older ones, can be about that gift.

Today is the day. They were all right. Blackie leads us to a door in the midst of the dead orchard, an old storm shelter, unused because it floods in the rain, and I lead Mary in.

Nobody will find us here. We'll be safe.

But you're not playing the game right. You're It. You're the only one looking for us.

It's not her fault she doesn't know.

The stench of mushroom rot is overwhelming, and I can't understand why the wind hasn't carried the trees away in its arms, why the lightning hasn't scorched the earth with its ozone love.

But my eyes are so heavy.

Are you okay?

Yes, Mary. Yes. I'm fine, I lie.

#

Mary is crying, shaking me, and a small-voice

woman is talking to her. I open my eyes, then shut them again to keep out the pain. We're still in the death rot mushroom box, but we're no longer alone.

Why is it so bright?

Mary stops shaking me. She drapes her body over me, and I feel her warm and fragile arms around me. *Lucy, I was so scared.*

Someone laughs, a sound as jagged as newly broken beer bottles in the sand, the kind that might slice an uncareful foot. *Lucy? Is that what the humans call you? Have you even told them what you are?*

I open my eyes, just a little bit, and look at the source of the voice. *You don't know what I am to mock me. You hide behind light, but I can smell that you, too, are a friend of time and death.*

The painful light dims. She stands before me, a glass-pale woman. Not white, but the absence of color, all distorted reflections of the room around us. She is beautiful and singular as an eel. My own costume seems a shabby mockery against her dress.

Mary lets go of me when I sit up. She hides behind me and peeks out at the thing. The woman. Whatever it is.

"What's your name, child?"

I shake my head no at Mary. *Don't tell her. She hasn't told you hers.*

"You can call me Oona." The same laugh when she says it. I thought she was small, but she's bigger than me, and closer than I want.

Don't tell her. You don't have to tell her.

I won't. Mary whispers it in my ear.

The smell of decay is strong enough I retch, dry. If I let fish go long enough to smell this way, we'd be dead on eating them.

I smell cookies. Mary whispers again.

Oona smiles, just at Mary, and laughs, just at me. Oona frowns and steps away when she sees me notice. I wasn't supposed to see both. She's so bright again I have to shut my eyes, even with my protection.

I want cookies. You promised a special present.

You just had cake and ice cream. What is it Bigman says? *If you eat more, you'll get fat like a whale. Nobody likes a fatso.*

Behind me, Mary sniffles. *But you promised.*

"I have cookies. Do you want to share?"

Eyes aren't needed to know where Oona is, even though the shelter is too big. Far bigger than when the door was opened. The stench of Oona, the silence of her is enough. She's holding her breath. I lunge at the place and slash. My hand connects, but my glove gets in the way. Fabric rips instead of flesh.

"Little girl, the cookies are all around. Just eat one."

Mary can't hear the danger in it. She smells of expectation. Risking my safety, I turn my back on Oona and grab Mary's arms. Even though the hole we're in is so bright it hurts, I look her straight in the face. *If you eat those, you'll die. They're mushrooms, not cookies. Mushrooms.*

Mushrooms are gross. Lucy, I want to go home. She starts crying again.

I know, Mary. I'll take you home.

Oona thinks she can creep up on me by plunging us into darkness. She can take the light, but she can't help her stench.

I leap at her, and my claws find her, but they're still foiled by fabric. This time, it's hers. I feel my claws snag and hear the tragic rip of fabric. For that alone, I'm owed blood.

You're making me ruin your dress.

What does he call you? What do you call him? The smell of trod soil tells me where she's gone. If I can keep her away from Mary, rescue Mary, open the door, I'll be the hero of today.

I call him John.

I can hear that's a lie. She kicks me hard in the leg, but she's not wearing shoes. It hurts more when people are wearing shoes.

I call him Bigman, all right?

Giving up a secret doesn't feel good, but maybe it will distract her. She tries to kick me again. This time I'm ready, and I wrench her ankle, pop pop pop. Ankles are always broken by three, if she's built like Bigman.

Oona screams, and behind me Mary whimpers in fright. The place smells of piss. Rot and piss.

The light comes back, but not as strongly. No light

comes from Oona's foot, even though it dribbles from the rest of her, and she limps back.

She smiles. This time for me. *They told me today was the day. I should have listened.*

The day for what? Why did nobody tell me they didn't mean Mary's birthday?

The day for you. Your birthday. Another year closer to the judgment.

I can kill her later, if I need. Bigman always says nobody knows when I was born. My parents abandoned me to the ocean.

You know me? Not just what I am, but who I am?

You are Dragon, the great enemy.

Nobody's my enemy unless they make themselves so.

Oona sits on the ground. She winces, and I'm glad.

What does he call you, this Bigman of yours?

I'm Knot.

That's what the great enemy always says. But who is to say that fate knows everything? Maybe it's different this time.

I sit without responding, my breath still ragged from our fight, Mary still crying behind me. After a while, Oona explodes into light, the after-image burning my eyes like the vague memory of a girl who should be there, and I can't smell her anymore.

#

It's dark outside when I lead Mary from the room, her sweaty hand in my ruined glove. Dogs are baying back and forth. *Girl? Girl? Girl? Find the girl!* Their voices are still distant, but the stench of spoor and markings is close. They've passed through here and will likely be back soon.

I want to go home. Mary's still sniffling.

The moon is the right brightness for a day to have passed. Either we were in that hole only a day or we were gone much longer. You only send dogs early and late. Early to find the people, late to find their corpses. A day, then.

Bigman has warned me about fairies, and now it's clear to me that Oona can't be anything else. Mary's lucky it wasn't years. *I'll take you home,* I tell her. Whatever storm was inviting itself in has departed, and the night is the pebbled blur of a cloudless sky. Mary follows me, not dragging behind this time, through the gray lands.

The sharp stink of cat cuts through the musted fur smell of the dogs. *Blackie, come out. I can smell you.* She slinks out, holding her tail high behind her. The broken end of it points away, a false finger of blame.

I tried to tell you it was the day, but you wouldn't listen. Her guilt has made her sloppy. She should have run before I escaped or kept her mouth shut and sworn it was an accident.

Maybe I should kill Blackie, but I don't have many friends, and I knew she was a cat when I met her. It wouldn't be fair to punish her for that nature now.

Do you serve the fairy, then? She bristles at the accusation, arches her back and hisses at me. Mary hides behind me, away from Blackie.

Careful, I warn the cat. *You hurt the girl, and I'll kill your whole family.* She relaxes, gives a friendly purr to put Mary at ease.

I didn't know it was a fairy. Bigman said to lead you there if you were acting strangely. Should I have ignored him?

It's not her fault, then, but that doesn't make it better. *Where is he now?*

Blackie shrugs in her cat way, rubbing herself against Mary's legs. She purrs loudly when the girl picks her up. *Last I saw, he was passed out at home. I left. Too many big people at your house.*

That means there's no chance he doesn't know I took Mary. Maybe he won't be mad. It seemed like the only choice when I did it, but now I suspect it was a fairy trap.

Some of my favorite shows have fairies who are kind and pretty and can fly. Not everything small is ugly and dangerous. But I've seen the other shows. I know about the dark fairies, too. The ones who steal teeth. The ones who steal souls, as if there were such things.

Come on Mary, I'll take you home. She nods and hugs Blackie tighter. Back we walk, through the dead orchard to the lighthouse.

The house is blazing. Sadly, it's only light, not fire, but enough that ships would be warned away even without a lamp. Everything stinks of dog, and the noise is overwhelming. *Don't see me*, I tell everyone and let go of

Mary's hand. As soon as I do, she starts crying, and a police woman is picking her up, Blackie and all.

Bigman broods on the couch. Even before I get close, I can tell it's him. He smells like anger.

When I bite a chunk from his ear, just enough to let him know that I'm angry too, he claps his hand to staunch the wound, and I can smell fear, though the anger smell doesn't go away. *You almost got Mary hurt. You almost got me hurt.*

Usually, I can't stand the taste of Bigman's blood. Today, though, it's opening something in me, letting it blossom like a corpse flower. I've only seen them on TV because Bigman would never take me to the jungle to see them.

"Oh, my Lucy has returned. Thank God," he cries out, Bigman, who has never thanked any god for anything.

Don't see me, I tell everyone, but Mary grabs my hand and everyone is looking at me now.

One of the women tells Bigman, "We'd like to interview your daughter, in case someone lured them away. Why don't you come with us?"

She doesn't look at me, even though she says she wants to talk. Bigman takes my hand, and Mary lets go. I can feel the bones of my fingers grinding against each other in his grip. He drags me upstairs to his office and sits me on a chair, then stands across the room to let the woman talk to me.

Hi. She says it as three syllables. *What's your name?*

What's yours? I demand. Too many people wanting to know names.

I'm Officer Bradbury. Her mouth smiles, but her scent says she's bored. She leans close enough that I worry she's going to hug me, but she just whispers in my ear. *Can you tell me what happened? If your daddy hurt you, you can just squeeze my finger.*

I shake my head at her. They don't know who Bigman is, not the way I do. He's certainly not my daddy, even if I don't know precisely what he is, and this is his fault. But it won't be them who punishes him.

I clamber down from the chair and go to Bigman. My arms are wrapped around his leg, and I push hard against the wound on his thigh, gripping more tightly until he smells like pain.

Seeing me love and love and love him, the officer decides everything is all right. She shakes Bigman's hand and then leaves.

Soon after, Mary's parents come and take her away. She doesn't even say goodbye.

#

I knew when I went to sleep that Bigman was angry. Even after I stitched his ear, he kept complaining that he wouldn't be pretty anymore. As if! That would be like me complaining the same. What use is beauty to us unlovable monsters?

I can smell him down there. The tang of whiskey is seeping in under my door, earlier than it usually does.

But now, the window won't open. I try the door, and it's locked. Twisting the knob doesn't open it, and even when I kick at it, I can't hear him coming to let me out.

The peacocks ought to be screaming their stupid heads off, and the crash of the ocean should be background music to the day, but I can hear nothing from outside the room.

Even when I turn my little TV all the way up, Bigman doesn't come to check on me. I could be lying here dead, and he wouldn't even care. Lucky for him, one of the good cartoons is on. Without him here to scold me, I sit close enough I can feel the crackle of the screen and see the details in the characters.

I should break the window is what I should do. He'd have to replace it, and he'd complain about how much it costs and how hard it is to make money when he can't leave the house much. Many times, people have come by wanting to buy his ruined kingdom, not caring what it looks like. They promise to tear it down and build something amazing. He could just say yes, and his money problems would be over. That he says no means he's a liar.

During the commercials, I run and jump at the window, but it rebuffs me. Once, twice, three times, and it still won't break. It must be making some noise outside because the kestrel comes to investigate. I can't hear what he's saying, and after a while he gives up and flies away. You can't trust a bird to do anything right.

If I were in Bigman's room, I could slash up his bed, pour out his drinks into his computer, get his attention. But what good would it do to ruin my own costumes or destroy my own TV?

When I hear scrabbling from the door, I ignore it. Bigman isn't going to fool me. He either opens the door or not, but tormenting me isn't going to work. *Open the door, coward!* I mostly ignore it.

There's lizard stink coming from somewhere, and when I get up to find it and shoo it away, the lizard that Blackie pulled from the bushes is here.

I saw you dead.

I wasn't dead. Cats are bad news, and I didn't want to be eaten.

How do you know I won't eat you?

Because I come with gifts. The kestrel told me you're trapped.

Don't you know kestrels eat lizards?

We're allies in the fraternity of the clawed.

It skitters back under the door, out of the room, but where it had been standing I see a smear of silver. Getting close, it's one of the scales.

When the lizard returns, I'm still searching for where the scale fits. There's the click of another scale being dropped. It takes an hour for the lizard to bring all of the scales, but I fit them to my hands.

In the distance, the peacocks are screaming, the surf is pounding, cats are talking. And I remember so much more, but still something is missing.

The lizard is cool in my hands when I pick it up and bring it to my face. *Thank you, little one. But I'm still missing one.* I can see the red border on my wrist marking the scale's proper place. Even if I couldn't, I know its absence by the holes in who I am. How many years have I been trapped here? Why have I let Bigman keep me, now that he is old and weak?

That's all there was.

I count them, and it's the same number as before, but my wrist is bloody and tender. *Where is the last one?* The lizard shrugs as lizards do and scurries down my arm and out the door.

Now, I can see the lines running through the window, lines like the kind meant to keep glass from shattering. They're weak things, suggestions meant for me that the window shouldn't be opened or broken or tampered with. They stink of Bigman. With my new hands, I rip out these ribbons of suggestion and stamp them underfoot. They are no more substantial than a cobweb.

The window opens easily without them in the way, and I climb down to the library window. The ribbons are there, too, but now that I can see them they're easy to remove.

Bigman sits at his computer, playing games as though he hasn't betrayed me. As though I am not his prisoner. *Don't see me,* I tell him. When I crawl up to his shoulder, the shifting of his chair tells him I'm there. He turns and looks, his face inches from mine. My claws rest on his cheek, just below one of his eyeballs.

Why'd you lock me up?

He stinks of piss and blood. He always stinks of blood, but he usually doesn't stink of piss until he's had far more to drink than I smell on him now.

You kidnapped a girl. You brought the police into our home. You think you can just do that without consequence?

She was in danger from the storm. I wasn't kidnapping her. But Blackie says you told her to lead me to the fairy.

What was I supposed to do, Knot? The fairy says she can restore the land with your help but that you'd never go willingly if you knew.

Where's the other one?

He looks at me in confusion, and the smell of him says he really doesn't know what I mean. I show him my hands, and his fear is sharp. I show him the spot where one scale is missing. *Where's the other one?*

He shakes his head. *I don't know. I didn't know it was ready yet.*

Ready?

To be taken. The fairy must have stolen it. I can help you get it back.

You better. Bigman can be useful. For now.

#

Bigman says he's eager to help me get the scale back, though I can hear trickery in his voice, like when he talks with people about their parties.

With only a bit of persuasion, he knows all about fairies. *They're crepuscular creatures, best able to touch our world at dawn and dusk. That's the best time to catch them without being caught yourself.*

Then how'd Oona find me so late in the day?

You must have eaten sugar, Bigman says. His sly look doesn't fool me into confession.

Why would that matter?

It takes down your walls. That's why you wandered off and got lost. But I can smell the lie of it. Just because they're walls inside me doesn't mean they're my walls. Someone has put them there, and Bigman has fooled me into caretaking them, like one of those birds that puts their babies in other birds' nests.

I'm hungry, and without me in the house to take care of things, Bigman has let us run out of food. Since I need to wait for dusk anyway to catch Oona, I dress to go fishing, with a fly fisher's vest and hat, rubber boots, and Bigman's pole over my shoulder.

We're going fishing.

You go ahead. I'm tired and in pain.

I'm not carrying the sack.

He sighs and whines, but he shuffles off to get dressed and then we head down to the beach. Today, I walk with him so he doesn't wander off and get lost. Two can worry about that for each other.

A faint breeze is licking at my neck, where the hat doesn't quite reach. *Windy today.*

Bigman flinches when I comment. *I don't feel it.*

Even before we get to the water, I can hear the shore birds playing, taunting each other with who has had the better day. One raucous fellow calls out his story, *and it landed right in the cup!* Up and down the shore, the other birds roar their approval. They're still screaming *cup cup cup* when we come to the surf.

I shed my clothes on the beach and enter the ocean. Let Bigman fetch them before the tide carries them away. I no longer care.

My scaled hands nearly glow in the water. I had worried the scales would dull my senses, the way clothes do when other people are around and Bigman insists I swim with them on, the way the goggles both protect and blind me. Instead, I feel every wave, feel the vortices pulled into being by the bigger creatures. When I put my head below the surface, oily rainbows hang above, where water and sky meet, showing where boats have been by recently.

You're imagining things. I know that's what Bigman would tell me. He's said it to me before when I've caught glimpses. But this is no imagining. Only the empty spot on my wrist feels incomplete. It drags when I stroke the water.

Come little fishies, see what I have in my bag.

Even before they arrive, I can hear them well enough to count them, to know how big they are. A fat, iridescent pompano arrives, swollen with eggs. *Not for you today*, I tell her. She lets me stroke her fins before she swims off in disappointment. More young fishes for later, if I leave the ones with eggs.

When my bag is full, a few mackerel are still lingering, hoping to get some of the goodies I've promised. Ravenous after my ordeal, I snatch two of them and eat them fresh. The fish in the bag panic, smelling blood, and the few unbagged nearby dart away. The slippery flesh is delicious, but not as good as after it's fried. I take my bag to Bigman.

Take them back and cook them up for us. He shouts for me to get out of the water when I head into the waves again, but even after a little more swimming I could beat him to the house. If the dogs eat him today, he's earned it many years gone. My concerns are more pressing.

Far south of my beach, I approach a mermaid pod browsing among the mangroves, alerting them to my presence long before I arrive and letting them know I mean no harm. Normally, they avoid me and stay silent, but only a few tides ago they knew the day was coming and said so.

I see you've found and fixed your flippers. She looks at my gorgeous hands. Her back is covered in deep grooves, her wounds ancient enough that moss fills them. She's the one who had twin calves last year. The others could be male or female, but I'm not romancing them, so I don't ask.

I'm missing one.

She comes closer to investigate my silvered hands. Her fleshy lips taste my claws without biting, tickling at the spot where a scale is missing, and I stroke her whiskers when she's done. *Few escape whole. You seem healthy enough despite your loss.*

I remember now that I'm Dragon. Do you know about us?

If anyone knew where he was, you could ask Leviathan. He knows everything worth knowing.

Leviathan?

She snorts in amusement. *A bit of a jumped-up whale, though his knowledge is vast. If he knows about the great serpent whose name he bears, he won't say. Though he might to you. A Dragon hasn't been seen in these waters within my grandmother's memory. She told us tales, but Dragon had been absent since before she was a child.*

So I'm the last?

Rising up, she paddles water down at me. A friendly mermaid laugh. *Or the first. Or not Dragon at all. You're awfully small.*

She surfaces for air, and I follow her up. The sun shows that it's late afternoon.

Where is Leviathan?

I told you already nobody knows.

Nobody?

Well, Bird might. But watch your neck if you seek out Bird.

Of course I'm going to find this Bird character. The name stirs a memory, but it's too common a word to evoke much.

Thank you. May your flippers ever find tender shoots instead of fishing lines, I call to her as I swim home to ready for meeting Oona at dusk. I didn't think about my farewelling before I took my leave, but I know it was the right thing to say.

#

Bigman is yelling at his computer when I get back, and the fish are dead in their bag in the kitchen, heads still attached. *You were supposed to cook them,* I remind him. *Are you coming with me to the fairy?* He ignores me.

No help for it, then. I head back downstairs to chop and fry them. The internet box is in my way, and I trip over it, and it accidentally comes unplugged. Upstairs, Bigman starts cursing.

Chop chop chop. Fry fry fry. I leave the extra bits in the sink, uncooked, and a few fried up for Bigman. Maybe Blackie will come by and pilfer them later. Maybe Bigman will have to clean them up before they stink.

Hot food inside me and the sun near the horizon, I put on a heavy motorcyclist's outfit. Bigman got it for me as a joke, because it's hot and heavy and *nobody would ever mistake you for someone tough.* It's just right for now, though.

If Oona has some sharp trick ready for me, the leather will act as armor.

Come with me like you promised. I give him one last chance before leaving. Outside, the heat is sweltering with me dressed so warmly.

Where you headed, Knot? Blackie is rubbing my legs as though she hadn't just betrayed me. I kick at her, but I'm slow, my heart not in it, and she dodges away. *You still sore about before?*

Shut up, I tell her. But now I feel bad for being mean. How would a cat know better? *I'm going to get my last scale from Oona.*

Even though she praised them before, Blackie bristles when she sees the change in my hands, and her pupils narrow to slits. *My family is calling.*

They're not. They're talking about how much they like you gone. They're going to steal the fish heads I left in the sink and not leave any for you.

Bigman says I shouldn't ever lie, even though he does, but I'm doing Blackie a favor. She didn't even know there were fish heads. And if Bigman hasn't calmed down and had dinner, maybe Blackie and her clan will take the fried bits, too, and Bigman will go hungry.

It hasn't been long since Blackie left, and here is the lizard, running alongside me as I walk. He's small but his smell is big. *You found a shell.* The approval makes me smile. I had been regretting my choice of clothes.

You never know when you'll need one. Why did you help me, before?

His slow lizard chuckle buzzes against my ears like the rustle of dried leaves. *You'll be the best one of us, when you remember everything. If you regard us scaled ones kindly, you can help us win against the furred ones. Not everything with claws is an ally.*

Closer than it seemed when I had to drag Mary behind me in flight, we find the door. *You coming with me?*

This is not my place. If you come out soon, I'll be here. He retreats into the dead brush.

The heavy door keeps trying to shut itself, so I take off my boots and use them to prop it open. The ground inside is soft and full of mushrooms, so I shouldn't need footwear.

Oona? Are you here? No answer. *You foul flutterbug, where are you?* Still no answer, and with the door open I can see that the room is small, just big enough to hold some gardening tools and bags of fertilizer. The mushrooms are growing from these bags.

When Mary and I were here, this place seemed endless and ancient. When Oona and I fought, I scuffled far beyond where the wall of this room ends.

Bigman says I can't watch horror movies because they might give him nightmares, but he doesn't check what I watch in my room. Maybe this is why the door always slams shut behind them. With the door open, you can't see the secret passages. The monsters can't get to you.

You can't get to the monsters.

I put my boots back on but hold the door open. The sun has nearly set, and the leafless trees are an army of angry spirits, marching off to fight the great fire. *Farewell, brave soldiers!* They don't respond, but I didn't expect them to.

Inside, I let the door shut behind me. It opens easily again when I try the knob. I check it three times before I trust I'll be able to leave.

The mushrooms are glowing dimly, and by their light I can see that the room has expanded. The picking stick, a long pole with a metal basket on the end and a claw for pulling down oranges, is a makeshift halberd in this space. I take it and wave it in front of me.

Oona? I've come for my scale. Give it back to me and nobody has to get hurt.

I can hear her breathing shallowly, near to the ground. It is the breath of a small and wounded animal. *You've come to finish me off, then?*

She gasps sharply when I nudge her with my boot. *Promise you won't try to hurt me*, I demand.

I promise, for whatever a fairy's word is worth.

My face close to hers, the reason for her pain is obvious. A long stripe of blood divides each cheek in two, and the dress she had been wearing is in tatters. Faint yellow light drips from her like yolk from a smashed egg. *I didn't do this. You were fine when you left me.*

Her laugh is tinny and doesn't have much heart in it. *Mostly fine*, she says.

Where is my scale?

My queen took it.

You gave her what belongs to me?

Not willingly. She gestures to the evidence of this truth.

Where is your queen? I'll take it back.

She reaches out and grasps my claws. I start feeling dizzy, then remember to breathe. There is no loathing in her touch, not the way there is when Bigman has to touch me. *My queen is beyond your reach, but not beyond reach.*

Will you die now? She and I could have been best friends. What happened before, the argument over that girl, need not have come between us.

She laughs. The sound of it is the smell of bitter almonds. *No, I will not die. I will merely suffer.*

How do I reach your queen?

Take my crown. It is the least I can do for the favor you'll owe. You'll know when to give it back, when you begin to serve the crown instead of the crown serving you.

It leaves her head without resistance and fits mine perfectly. Though it is gold in color, it is barely thicker than fishing line. Only magic could make it hold its shape and let it fit both of us. *If you're not the queen, why do you have a crown?*

Among the fairies, we're all queens. Only a few of us have other fairies as our subjects.

I leave her in the dark. The door opens easily. The lizard is gone.

At home, Bigman doesn't mention my crown, but he's cleaned up the fish mess. He's learning.

Chapter Four

The sun is not even up yet, though the tide is full, and Blackie is batting at my claws, clearly intent on waking me. *What?*

You'll want to come with me.

Because you've been so loyal? But I get up anyway. Blackie often invites herself places, but she's never invited me anywhere before, except to the fairy. She wouldn't be foolish enough to try that again, would she? If it's Oona's queen, I wouldn't complain. My hands are itching toward action.

I was worried that I wouldn't be able to sleep with the scales on, or that I would scratch myself while I was asleep, but I feel more alive than I can ever remember feeling without them. It's too early for the peacocks and their cacophony, but I can hear fishing boats in the distance and animals moving in the pre-dawn.

Milk? Blackie has ever been a beggar, but I pour her some milk anyway. It means there won't be enough for Bigman's tea, but he can do without. Milk doesn't belong in tea. Even now, the regular wheeze of his sleep is clawing its awful way around the house, up my tower and back down to the kitchen.

What are we doing, Blackie?

We're going to the cat town.

I rummage through my closets and find a costume from the before time, old enough I don't remember if Annea or Bigman gave it to me, and dress myself as a cat. Blackie and I are almost twins, though my tail just flops behind me and my claws are sharper and silver.

Looking closely, there are tendrils of black along my hands. *Could they become black to match my costume?*

As soon as I think it, I see that they do match the costume. They're still smooth, not fuzzy, but when I look at them the patterning makes them appear to be covered in fur. Bigman would be so jealous. I've seen him play as a cat person when the internet isn't working, and he always complains that he can't make his paws match his armor. *I'm better than him in this.*

Blackie peers up at me. *Better than whom?*

I stroke her back and scratch her ears. *No matter.*

The morning is warm already, and the moon's brightness is enough to see Blackie moving ahead of me. The cat leads me away from Mary's house, toward the property in the other direction, where the wedding was. Where Annea used to live.

After a few minutes, we reach the edge of the

blight. Blackie slinks beneath a low hedge, and I push through after her.

We skulk, two predators not yet in need of breakfast, across a driveway and to another orchard, one that's not dead. I can hear more cats, not far away, and their odor is thick in the air, but not unpleasant.

When cats stink, they do it to punish the animals around them. A shelter, like the one where Oona was hiding but without its door, is the source of the sound and the smell. Blackie darts into it, and I follow her.

Unlike the dank hole where Oona had been hiding, the tunnel here is short, and it soon opens into a full town. I saw the cartoon where there's a cat town that's just like a people town, but this isn't like that. The roof is still close enough to my head that I can reach it if I jump. Bigman would have to lean over even more than usual to walk through here without bumping himself.

Small windows let light out from buildings that line the streets. I look inside one and see a pair of cats snoozing by a small fireplace, but Blackie pulls me away.

Rude, she says. *Don't stare in windows.*

Soon we leave the neighborhood. Cat houses are much smaller than regular houses, and certainly smaller than the lighthouse, so it doesn't take much time. In the center of a large open area is a fountain, with light from Christmas bulbs strung along the ceiling. Instead of a statue, there is only a pipe in the middle, but water shoots softly from it at several different heights, falling into a pool that slowly drains itself.

Are you stealing this water? I look suspiciously at Blackie. Maybe they're what's wrong with our fountain.

You can't steal water. Water belongs to everyone. Might as well ask if we're stealing air.

I thought cats lived in the forest and stuff, I said. *I didn't know you had plumbing.*

Blackie sniffs, offended. *Certain kinds of cats like living outside, but there are also civilized cats.* When Blackie says civilized, we hear another pair of cats yowling and hissing. It's been a constant sound since we arrived, and it doesn't seem very civilized to me.

Wait here, Blackie says. I sit on the edge of the fountain. It's only a little bit low for me, so my feet can easily reach the ground. The light is too dim to see much of my reflection, but I know it would be smiling back at me.

#

Blackie comes back soon and offers me a fish. We haven't been down here for very long, but it would seem rude not to take it, and she's taken enough fish from me that she couldn't possibly expect a debt for it. I brush the fur off of it and eat it raw. Bigman thinks raw fish is gross, but some of the Japanese cartoons show people eating it with rice, so he's just an unhappy man about that. It doesn't make me weird that I like them fried or raw.

Singly and in pairs and small groups, hundreds of

cats come into the square. They rub themselves against my legs, and some of them let me pet them with my scaled hands. I can feel their silky fur as well as I could before I got my scales back, but when a few of them put their paws in my hand, their extended claws don't scratch me at all.

The area around me is getting full, and each new cat has to wend its way through a crowd now to reach me. Though the cats are mostly quiet, enough of them are here that I can feel a deep thrum in the air, as though I'm inside an even bigger cat, and it's purring.

Hundreds of cat eyes are staring at me, but they turn almost as one to look at a new arrival. It's obvious this is who is in charge. A calico, her ears rising as high as my shoulders, lounges through the assembled cats, who move out of her way like she's parting the waters to guide her people to safety. A procession of others tend to her. Her eyes are different colors. Each eye watches me on its own, as though she were two cats doing loving battle while guarding against interference.

She chuckles, and her voice is deeper than a dog's. *I appreciate the respect of your proper dress, Dragon. You have my permission to wear your crown in my presence, which is something not lightly granted.*

I reach up and feel it. The crown is light and comfortable, like it has always been part of my hair. I had forgotten I was wearing it.

My granddaughter says you're rebelling against the big man, the fisher king.

Blackie, I met your grandmother. This isn't her. What's going on? Blackie hisses at me and bats tentatively at my leg. I bend down to let her whisper.

Knot, the queen is everyone's grandmother. You're lucky she's granted you an audience, so please be polite.

It never hurts to be polite, despite what Bigman says, that *only weaklings and beta males follow rules.* Here is a queen. Bigman is no king in this court. At best, he would be a fallen knight who lies about being in charge. I see that now.

I am in rebellion, I confirm, and by saying it make it so. *What is your name, queen, so that I can address you properly?*

Are you prepared to reveal your name, Dragon?

I'm Knot.

And just as you wisely keep your true name from me, I will keep my own name private. But I grant to you a boon, if you will promise me a favor, one monarch to another.

I look at Blackie to see what she thinks, but she has eyes for her queen only. Missing a scale, I can feel that I'm missing memories, but I didn't realize I was missing a name. If Knot is not my true name, what should I be called? I have gotten no letter from a school for dragons, nor met any others. What kind of names would they have?

I am no monarch. Neither queen nor king. But I make you a promise as myself. On my friends' lives, I will owe you a favor. It's not much of a promise when you have no friends.

Very well. The queen begins convulsing, making the horrible noise that cats make when they call forth hairballs. It's their fault for licking themselves all the time. What comes up is no hairball, though. It is a jet black pebble that glows softly, sucking light from the air around it. She puts her paw on it and pushes it toward me. *Swallow it,* she says.

I pick it up and swallow it. Blackie leads me out the door, through the crowd, past the neighborhood. All of the lights are dark, and I can smell the memory of cats but none other than Blackie seem to be there when I look back. They must have all come to see the queen. Blackie stops when we get to the opening that leads outside. *Don't come back here without an invitation,* she says.

I'm not allowed?

Blackie stretches herself and flexes her claws. *It's just not a good idea. We stayed in the areas that are safer. There are some bad cats in town, even if they behave when they know the queen has a guest. And there's the cat alley, which is some place you never want to find yourself even though all cats go there eventually. Just, it's better if you only come when invited.*

I go home alone. The pebble is burning its way through my body, but the warmth makes me feel ecstatic, not alarmed. It's enough to overcome my disappointment that I didn't get to explore the cat town, only come to its doorstep.

Maybe I'll be invited back later. If not, I know where to find them. Who is Blackie to tell me I'm not welcome?

At home, Bigman is watching TV on the big screen. I take the remote and put on cartoons.

I was watching that! He grabs for the remote, but I'm faster.

You've seen that one before.

You don't know that. He's pouting.

I've seen it before, so I know you have. I don't like your shows.

He grumbles, but he knows I'm right. Soon, he goes to the kitchen and I smell him cooking fish. Before my show is even over, he brings it out and sets a plate in front of me. He's made it too spicy, but it's still good. *Nom nom nom.*

Have some manners. He hands me a napkin, and I wipe my mouth. I flick out my tongue to show him it's clean.

You want more?

I nod hungrily, and he fills my plate again. The show ends, and he brings me even more.

I'm feeling sleepy. So so sleepy.

Too sleepy! *You drugged me?* As though I've never seen a movie! I'm wide wide awake now, flooded with the need to fight. I leap at one of him, but they're both much faster than me, and I stumble.

It's for your own good. There he is. I lunge, but he trips me, and my face hits the floor and my claws skitter along it. Bigman's going to be so mad about the scratch when he sees it.

There's pressure on my back. His knee. *You're going to regret this!*

I'm goiba regrepdis? You're not making sense. Quit struggling and you won't get hurt.

He wrenches one arm behind me, and I feel a pressure on my wrist. Then he wrenches the other one back, too, and I can't move. He's tied me up.

You better not ever let me go, or I'm going to kill you.

That's the problem, you think you're in charge, but you're Knot. He picks me up and throws me onto the couch. I didn't think he was strong enough, so it catches me off guard, which is the only reason he manages it.

I could escape, but I'm feeling so sleepy, and the couch is so soft.

Oh, here's Bigman.

He's got a knife and his stupid cup. His *chalice*, his *grail*, he calls it. More wasted money money money. I start laughing and it's hard to stop.

The grail is on the coffee table in front of me. We don't even drink coffee! He doesn't like it, and *it would stunt your growth*. But we've got a coffee table.

When he drags the knife along his palm and starts his ridiculous bleeding, it just makes me laugh harder. *Drip drip drop drop* into the cup.

But oh ho ho, that trick won't work on me. He slashes my palm with the knife and it just makes a scraping noise. *Magic!* I yell it at him. He's lucky I don't go super saiyan and explode everything with fire. Bigman doesn't like that show.

The knife won't come out of his hand, even with me grabbing blindly at the blade. My hands are tough like gauntlets now. *Watch out watch out! I'm gonna get ya!* Soon enough, I'll work my hands out of these ropes.

You should see the look on his face. I haven't seen him this scared and angry since he got fragged by his own team online and screamed death and vengeance for hours.

But *Ow!* I can feel he's cut my arm, above the scales. *Not funny!* It was more surprising than it is painful. *Drip drip drop drop* into the cup for my blood, too.

His face is so so close to mine. The hair sneaking out of the moist caves of his nostrils is thick and white. How come I never noticed?

I bind you by blood, he whispers, and makes me drink from the cup. He sets it down and reaches for me like when he makes me swallow medicine, pinching my nose and holding my mouth so I have to swallow. *There's no need for that.* I show him my empty mouth. If medicine were as tasty as blood, we'd never argue about it, even if I was sick.

He drinks too, and makes a yuck face. Guess he doesn't like it.

I bind you by blood, Bigman whispers again. He won't stop staring. *I bind you by blood. You may not harm me. You must obey.*

As if!

Bigman's not a smoker, so the lighter surprises me. He never lets me play with them, but now he's playing. I snap my jaw at it, but he snatches it away. *Click click click*, and he makes fire.

The chalice is flaming, our blood is burning.

I bind you by fire. I bind you by fire. I bind you by fire. You may not harm me. You must obey.

He unties my hands, and I try to rub feeling into them. My arm has a little blood still on the skin, and I lick a finger and rub the blood. The skin is unbroken beneath.

That wasn't very nice, I tell him. I hope it doesn't hurt his feelings. *Can I go to bed? I'm feeling sleepy.*

He smells like panic abated. *Go to bed. And forget about this*, he tells me.

That's all I want to do, but the crown is so tight on my head it hurts. I'll never forget this.

#

I have not forgotten.

My head hurts. I climb onto the bathroom vanity and look at it in the mirror. There's a thin circle of blood oozing down from where my crown touches my head, but no matter how much I tug, the crown won't come off.

Maybe I *should* gut him. More trouble than it's worth. I could just leave him here, safe, and go to find my scale. The rest of my stolen self.

Except I try the window, and it won't open. I leap against it, and it barely even wobbles. There's a thick line of chalk around it. Not *my* chalk.

Bigman! I stomp stomp down the stairs. *See me coming and be afraid!*

He's playing his game, and he doesn't even look up when I come into the room. Maybe I should just let him enjoy himself. There's no need to fight.

I get dressed, today as a butterfly, and head downstairs to go out and catch breakfast, but the front door won't open. Chalk there, too. Maybe there's something in the refrigerator.

In the kitchen, Bigman has left a mess. The chalice is on the counter, unwashed. Why would I let him get away with this? Of course there's reason to fight. His knife is there, too, but it's a small and pitiful thing. The cleaver will do much better.

When he sees me with it, Bigman has the decency to be afraid, to get up from his chair and aim it so that it is between us.

Put down the knife! he commands. I keep hold of it, though his words make my head hurt. Against my rational self, I step forward.

Stop where you are! His words hurt me, but an animal yowling inside me spurs me forward another step. If I am a butterfly, I am a carnivorous one. He wants to drink *my* blood? I will suck his veins dry of their nectar. A trickle of blood runs down my face, and I wipe it off with my hand, then lick my fingers clean.

He's finally afraid. *You are forbidden to hurt me!*

Why'd you tie me up? Why'd you drug me? That was so mean. I try to take more steps, to get within striking distance, but I can't push myself any further forward. Dropping the knife lets me crawl a little closer, but I'm stopped in even that.

Just because I can't reach melee distance doesn't mean he's safe. The cleaver flies toward him, launched by his betrayal of me, but he dodges it easily.

Why'd you tie me up?

He looks at me like I'm the wounded animal. He smells like pity. It's a vile stench.

You don't know what you're doing. I'm just trying to keep you safe. Why don't you let me hold your scales for you, and we can just go back to the way things were?

But they're mine. Not just you, but all of the others, too. They're not just mine, they're me. *You said you'd help me get the stolen one.*

He smells like shame. That, more than anything, cools my anger. I approach to see him better, to look at the expression on his face, and nothing stops me. Not like when I was aimed at hurting him. *You don't know how, do you?*

His eyes are wobbly like jellyfish.

You've got to stay safe, little one. This is for your own good.

I pick up the cleaver and take it back to the kitchen. I wash the dishes. He's a broken old man, and here I am, an ingrate, and a violent one at that.

Upstairs, and I'm watching TV. *This is wrong.* I should be out catching fish, but the windows won't open. The door won't open. Bigman has trapped me here, and even my mind is turned against me. If it weren't for the pain the crown is causing, would I just watch my shows until I starve?

I can't stay angry at Bigman. I try. He *deserves* my anger, but I can't do it. But I'm still angry.

From outside, I can hear a storm approaching, and I cheer it on. *Come rage with me!* I call out to it through the glass. Lightning blinks at me in reply.

The servant obeys, howls the wind.

I put my palm against the window. When I push, the window resists me, but I can feel its coolness and vibration against my scales. The glass is singing back to the wind.

Tear it all down, I demand.

The walls thrum in sympathy with the crash of waves. The peacocks scream in alarm, but they're cowards. They hide behind their size and chase a small one like me with their vicious beaks. The mermaids sing, asking me to calm myself, but they don't love me as much as I hate being captive.

I can hear Bigman yelling at me from far away, but I'm riding the storm clouds. My body might be in front of him, but my soul is high above, whipping the world into frenzy.

Just because I can't kill him doesn't mean he can't die. A storm plays no favorites. It has no targets, only victims. It does not break the rules. A storm is beyond rules.

#

Not yet at full tide, I break against the mangroves, ebb down the inconstant sand, slosh the fish around, and find the strength to surge again. Wave by wave *hush hush* I probe at the edges of the pretty lighthouse. *It will be our secret*, I promise.

But it wasn't a secret when Annea's brother drowned. Everyone found out, and everyone blamed me. I was the hero of that story, trying to save him, trying to warn him away from the deeper water. But I wasn't enough of a hero then. It's because Bigman had stolen the pieces of me. Each of my pieces remembers being stolen and locked away, now that they're returned to me. Except the one. Surely that one will hold the last of the secrets I'm being kept from.

Annea's brother, whatever his name was, was smaller than even me, but only because he was five. It was his fault for coming to swim with us. I never wanted him there. Annea didn't want him there. Only his parents thought him coming was a good idea.

You don't live by the shore and not learn to swim if you've got any sense in you. Or at least, you don't go swimming before you really know how to swim. Annea had brought her floaters with her like she usually did, but left them on the beach. I could always outswim her and she said it made her tired even though she practiced swimming at school. But he was gone so quick.

The tide had been coming in. I remember that always, because Annea couldn't go swimming when the tide was headed out. Her parents would look it up instead of just sniffing the air to know where the sea was at, what tricks it was up to. They thought a rising tide would carry us back to shore if we got too tired, or keep the sharks away, or something. Magic superstition.

The mermaids had come out to play in the surf. I had called them over for Annea to see them. They were shy like always, not saying anything. Too far for me to see them except as blobs, they were near enough that she was yelling at them in excitement. "Manatee! Manatee! Manatee!"

Of course they ignored her, when she wasn't even calling them by their right names. But that whooping and hollering had made her brother try to swim out to us, even though he usually just stood and let the waves break over his shins, giggled at the feel of the sand between his toes.

Annea looked back to the shore, wanting him to see the mermaids. "Where is he? He was standing right there!" She smelled worried.

I couldn't see the shore well enough to have spotted him anyway, so there was never a chance I could help, but I swam back anyway.

Annea yelled for him, but there was no answer. We

ran back to her house. She got there a long time before me because I was a better swimmer but she was a better runner. He wasn't there either, so it was run back down to the water, where we should have stayed in the first place.

I dove under and tried to smell him, but all I could smell of people was me and Annea. Even though I'd already done more than I should have had to, I swam back and forth across the bottom while the tide came in and dragged sand toward the beach, where it would sit and eat at the sea.

We never found his body, but Annea's dad pretended he'd died. He and Annea pretended the boy had died, and they blamed me for it.

"He only came because he had a crush on you," his father accused me. It was a lie. Nobody has ever had a crush on me. He was only five. Humans barely even know how to tie their shoes at that age, and I had done nothing to say I was interested in him romancing me. Five-year-olds don't know about romance unless their parents teach them.

I was no royalty, and he was no prince.

When his father punched me, not the stop-that slapping of Bigman but a punch like a boxer beating up a dead cow, I fell, bleeding. "Get out of here, monster. Freak. Don't ever come back here."

Still dizzy from his hit, I didn't fight him back. Not until later. But this all happened a long time ago. It is only the pain in my head making me think these things I want to forget. The storm is still coming at my call. Annea and her family are long gone, but I can smash it all anyway.

Feel my fury! I yell it as the storm.

Now, the tide fully in, the house yields instead of breaking. There is an entrance below the floor of the laundry nook, leading through fat pipes to caves in the sea. Bigman has overlooked the opening as too small for notice. The music of it echoes up through the lighthouse, but he never listens.

Exhausted, I release the storm. My butterfly wings droop.

Bigman creeps in and carries me tenderly to bed, and though he stinks of worry when he cocoons me in my blankets, he doesn't know I'm beyond that metamorphosis. I dream of escape.

Chapter Five

I wake at dawn, and Bigman is still up, playing on his computer. He gives me a dirty look, as though he were the one who had been wronged.

That storm brought a tree down on the neighbors' house.

Mary's house?

Other neighbors.

So I don't see why I ought to care. They can repair it good as new. You can't fix people once they're broken, but you can fix buildings.

The door and windows are still forbidden to me.

Let's go catch fish. I'm hungry.

Have some bacon and eggs. It doesn't have to be fish every day.

It was worth a try. Today I will leave on my adventure. I will stop in the fairy kingdom and pick up my scale, then go make my way in the world and see what Dragon trouble I can find. There's no reason to go on an empty stomach, though.

Long ago, back when Annea used to come over,

Bigman taught me how to cook. I think mostly he got tired of having to cook for me. Or disgusted at seeing me eat the fish raw, even though lots of people like sushi.

So it's not like I don't know how to make myself some food. Cartoons are always advertising for cereal, but Bigman claims it would just make me sick, even the stuff that says no sugar. He doesn't believe in easy. But we have some vegetables, which I'm not going to eat, and also some meat and eggs, which are delicious.

Maybe because I had such terrible sleep, or because someone decided to lock me up, I'm feeling clumsy when I make breakfast. There were a dozen eggs, and I cook six for myself. The others I accidentally drop. The bacon, too, when I've had my fill I can smell that the rest has been contaminated, so I throw it away. I wouldn't want Bigman to get sick. He'll be lost enough without me.

The pipe will be wet, but I know that when I reach land again, I'll need clothes. People get upset when they see me without them, and from how pretty Oona's dress was, I wouldn't want to be naked with the fairies. At least, I think that was a dress. In most of the shows with fairies, they're always wearing the same clothes. Do you think they get bored with them? What if fairy dresses are like their skin, the way penguins are always wearing tuxedos?

When I gave my princess dress to Mary, I didn't know I would be needing one so soon, but searching my closets I find the yellow dress from the movie where they torture the beast into giving up and becoming a man. It's pretty enough that it will do for my visit to the fairy queen.

With only a little work, it fits inside a big freezer bag. It's enough protection that I feel confident it won't get wet. Into my bag it goes.

Bigman deserves one last chance to be reasonable. I've been reasonable with him, so I'm hoping he'll do the same with me.

I'd like to leave now. He just glares at me and goes back to his game. He's looking sleepy, though.

Finally, he goes to bed.

He can be tricky. The first time he starts snoring, I jump on his bed and he wakes right up. I knew he was faking.

Two times now he hasn't woken, even when I bang pans.

I carry my sack downstairs and set it next to the washing machine. The washer must weigh more than I do. We've never had a new one, so it's decades old. Probably you could hide from a bomb inside. It doesn't budge at all when I push it. The hole below it is obvious, now that I know what I'm looking for.

A washing machine will not outsmart me. Even if it had an internet connection, that's not what they mean by smart machines. Bigman doesn't let me do the laundry because I don't do it right. It's hard to reach down and grab all the clothes out when they're done. I don't use the right amount of soap. Everything I do is bad and useless to Bigman.

But he's asleep and can't stop me. Today my wrongness will be useful.

His favorite leather jacket is the heaviest clothing we have, and I stuff it into the machine and turn on the water.

Twenty nervous minutes having passed, my excitement at escape growing, the spin cycle starts, and the washing machine starts walking around. *Thump thump thump*. It's easy to push it now, just nudging it the same direction each time it bounces, until it reaches the edge of its little platform and tips over with a *crash*. The hole is exposed.

My body is a little too big, something that almost never happens, and my skin is getting scraped up trying to fit.

Just relax and breathe slowly. It's a tight fit, but I promise the entrance is big enough. It doesn't have to hurt unless you make it. Inch by inch, I make progress through the narrow opening. It widens inside, enough that I can get my arms down past my waist. I grab my bag and bring it down with me.

Even at night, the ocean waters are lit from above by the stars and lit from below by the fish. Here, there is neither, and I am crawling along in the dark. I should have brought a flashlight, but I'm not willing to force myself back out and into my prison, so I push onward.

The slime below my fingers is just wet seaweed and lint. *The stink is lying to you*, I tell myself, knowing I'm a liar.

That isn't sewage, just laundry water. The commercial better not have been lying about the bags protecting from smell, or my dress is going to be foul.

It's taken forever, but here is the end of the pipe, this thing that has just banged my head. My claws show that it's a grating, like the drain on the shower. I turn around and kick at it, but it doesn't budge.

So now I am stuck here. The whole adventure ruined and useless. I grab the grating in my righteous fury and squeeze my hand closed.

With a shriek like a little girl screaming, the metal crumples and breaks, but my scales protect me. It is only twenty waves of the sea to rip the grating entirely free of the pipe.

I wait until I can hear water below me. From its echo, I am in a small cave and the water is only the height of a tree away. I jump, trailing my dress in its bag behind me.

I am free.

#

I told you it was the day.

The kraken is here, in the dark cave, taunting me with his octopodal squelches.

Show yourself, I demand. His body brightens, not so much it's painful but enough I can see he's lingering at the edge of a tide pool.

This place doesn't belong. The ground is covered in black glass, the volcanic kind they love on the nature shows. The beach near the lighthouse is white sand, silt.

Tell me how to get to the fairy queen. I need my scale before I can get on the road.

He shrugs his tentacles. *That's walker business.* I could hurt him, make him spill his inky secrets, but I was only hoping. Only a fool would think he knew the way.

Shine bright. By his light, I check to see that my dress isn't getting wet. It seems fine, so I rinse the bag.

The little monster is being petulant. *Rude! I didn't come into your house and dump garbage.*

Tell me how to get out of here, then.

Back the way you came? You didn't listen before, so why would you listen now? You're better off going back.

I'm no fool, though. I know that the waves coming in mean that there is some way out. I wade into the water and find where the waves are strongest. That means they weren't getting swirled around by bouncing off walls.

The bag makes it more awkward to swim, but I'm strong enough in the water that I make progress in the dark, swimming against the surge as it comes in, letting it pull me as it goes back out.

The kraken joins me. I knew he was a curious beast. Curiosity gets even the best of us. By his faint light, I have more confidence in my path. There is a long tunnel underwater. This area is wrong for lava tubes, but it reminds me of the ones I've seen on TV. Something burned through into here once, or maybe out of here, glassing the sand and leaving this tunnel.

We are twisting and turning and swimming for eternity. My shoulder is sore from pulling the bag behind me. I should have chosen a backpack, but maybe I would have been carried back by the force of the waves if I had.

Is it much longer?

Almost there, the kraken reassures me.

The end of the tunnel is bright, close to the surface and sunshine. When I break the surface, I can't see the lighthouse, but I can smell mangrove trees to the south.

I'm going to find the fairy, I tell the kraken.

So you say.

You can't trust a monster to be encouraging.

I swim forever and ever, but when I reach the mangroves they're not the right ones. The sun is burning low in the late afternoon sky, and this is the wrong place, but there's no helping it.

My dress is wrinkled, but the bag has kept it mostly dry. I put it on. It's just a little damp from being unwrapped. The hem drags in the moist sand, but looking back I can't see a trail behind me.

Too late, while I am still wet from the afternoon rain, I recognize the sound of peacocks. Usually, I hear them in the mornings, and I forgot their late-day stealth.

Die! Die! Die!

The birds are running screaming at me, tails shaking, many eyes staring at me. Up close, their screaming sounds like the girl's did, when she got sad but before she went away. Like Annea's did. I can't keep forgetting her name. If I can get the stolen piece of me, I'll remember for sure.

I turn to run from noise and memory, but my beautiful dress is heavy and awkward. There's no help for it but to fight.

Go away go away! I scream it back at the bullies, and they stop out of my reach. They scratch at the ground with their wicked claws, but I have claws now, too.

Die? The biggest screams it once. It almost sounds like a request.

You die, I have things to do. I glare back, even though I know the group of them could overwhelm me.

When one of them pushes through the group, small and brown, I breathe slowly, counting the breaths the way Bigman showed me.

The voices of the big males are familiar from their morning taunt. I'm far south of where I thought I was, but at least now I know.

Such pretty, the hen says. I haven't met her before.

My yellow dress is still wet, and I feel bedraggled, with sand still clinging to my feet. I should have brought shoes of some kind. My hair never bears mentioning, but it's short enough that it's hard to tell the difference between newly combed and a mess.

You're very pretty, too, I tell her. She squawks in amusement.

Pretty boys. Pretty boys. Behind her, they start preening. *Pretty pretty*, she says, and bobs her head at my claws.

Cautiously, I hold out my hands to her, and she rubs her head against them, the crown of her feathers folding down, dragging against my palms, and rising back up after it's passed through my hands.

Now that they've stopped trying to kill me, I need to be on my way. *I have to go find the fairy queen*, I tell her. I back away from them. It will be a long walk, but I know how to get back home now. I'll avoid the lighthouse itself. Bigman never leaves it anyway.

Come! Come! The hen tells me, and then all the others join in, too. *Come! Come!* They surround me.

Having no choice, I follow them deeper into the trees.

#

They herd me through the woods for what seems like hours. Each time I try to turn back or go a way they don't like, they start yelling at me again. When they get close, I take swipes at them, but they're fast and have both claws and a beak. My teeth would just get stuck in their feathers, I think. I could force an impasse, but not escape.

All of a sudden we're free of the trees and there is a house in front of us. At least, it would be called a house in fairy tales. Bigman would call it an eyesore, and demand the city make the neighbors tear it down. I've seen him do that, and quietly stop his noise when the neighbors gave him a little money. For his troubles.

If the witch from Hansel and Gretel was going to build a house of regular materials, instead of candy, this is the kind of place she would have.

Location would be a problem, but that's the last thing the TV shows about fixing up your house and making it easier to sell would mention about the house. The windows are so clean that they look like pieces of reflected sky from a distance, and the wooden fence around the garden is sand white, changing to wire partway up and curling over to form a roof.

When the peacocks leap up and sit on top, looking hungrily down at the greenery within, I see the wisdom in such a fence. The birds would devour everything there if allowed. Such rude and greedy beasts. I could forgive them that if it weren't for all of the screaming they do. Nature shows want to pretend peacocks are noble and beautiful. A costume can't hide a monster, though. I've learned that.

Up close to the house, the illusion is easy to see through. The roof is like the beach after a storm, covered in vegetation in various states of decomposition. Even from the ground, I can smell it. I can smell the sharper scents, too, indicating that the peacocks are not fastidious when it comes to where they aim.

I walk around the cottage. House is too grand a word for it. Vines try to trip me whenever I get too near the walls. There is only one door, on the side where the hen first left the woods. At least I'll know the direction to escape, if it comes to that, know how to get close enough to the sea to find my way to freedom.

The birds are becoming increasingly upset that I'm not headed to the door, and so, urged forward by the hen, I climb the two shallow steps to the front door. *Knock! Knock!* She yells it at me, and so I knock. The knob is low, within easy reach for me. The creak of a newly unburdened chair and a muttered profanity come from inside the house.

The door opens with a squawk of its hinges.

This person before me is not a child, though it takes me a moment to recognize that. They are only my height, but their eyes speak of endless years. The bony talons of their hands seize my shoulders. *Come in. I've been waiting for you.*

I am not the sort of creature that one waits for, unless it is with dread. Bigman has explained this to me before, that always I am an unwelcome guest. So unwelcome that when I tell people not to see me, they are delighted to oblige. That part, I discovered on my own. I think Bigman has figured it out, but we've never talked about it.

When I don't move from the doorway, merely breathe and blink, the person pulls me inside. Not roughly, the way one might yank a child back and clap a hand over her mouth lest she scream and alert the killers or the cops. It depends on what kind of mood Bigman is in when he chooses the movie.

The person pulls me in gently, as though I were a friend.

No matter where I look, the furniture is sized for me. The table is not so high that I have to clamber into a tall chair to reach. The sink, gleaming steel, rises only to my waist. I rush around the room, checking everything.

There are no other rooms. This single one is the entire nest, the kitchen, the bedroom, everything. There are three doors: one to a bathroom, one to the outside, and one to a closet that smells of seeds and roots and earth.

Do you want some tea?

The question is distracting, but I nod. I'm not sure I even like their kind of tea, but it would be rude to turn it down. In the movie, the dishes sang their invitation, but of course that won't happen here.

Even so, it's disappointing when a cup is set in front of me without even a melody.

Who are you? They seem to know me, but I don't know them. Adults don't usually answer this right. Sometimes they'll give a name, but names say so little about us.

I want to tell you a story, they say. Finally, someone answering the right way.

#

Some say that Chaos arose even before the world was young and hot, and that all of the old ones are his descendants. Others say that Night is the ancient mother. I say that Hope is the oldest of them all. Hope did not cower in Pandora's box, as in the legend you may have heard. Instead, Hope endured and gave birth to everything worthwhile.

Be that as it may, we may never agree on what gave rise to life. We can agree that something did, of course. That I, of all beings, am here to tell you, of all beings, this story makes it certain. Just as you are Dragon, I am Bird, and I have told you this story before.

I shake my head at them. *I don't know you.*

Bird smiles at me, and laughs. No teeth peek out from those jaws. The lips cover a hard beak that could probably crack wood, seed, and bone. They turn their head side to side, looking at me first with their left eye and then their right.

You don't remember knowing me. It's not surprising, given how small you are, and how young your body is. How little of yourself you have conquered. But hush while I tell the story. You can ask your questions after.

When Bigman tells me to shut up it just makes me angry, and I yell and stomp until he takes it back. Bird does not smell like one who would take it back. Despite the seeds and the roots in the cottage, Bird's breath smells of blood and meat. Peacock plumage decorates the walls and hangs from the exposed rafters. The scent of feathers lingers over the bed and the cushions. I shut up.

At the start, there was only one of each thing. The first amoeba is still alive, divided and twisted and changed over time, like all of us. Multitudes contain it.

There was only one Bird, and I am that one. This old body is not the one that soared over the continent before it split itself, but it contains Bird nonetheless. There was only one Dragon, and you are that one. You simply don't remember.

I shouldn't interrupt, I know, but Bird isn't talking sense. *But people are different. Bigman is not the girl. He is not the one who caused her sadness. Oona is not the fairy queen, who stole my scale.*

Bird shrugs the way a vulture does when it is hopping along the ground toward a fresh carcass, head bobbing down as shoulders rise up. Bigman doesn't like the bloodier nature shows, but as long as I promise not to act them out, he still lets me watch them.

He shouldn't have trapped me. I need to stop thinking about him. He'll starve to death soon, all alone, with nobody to make sure he eats or sleeps. But he shouldn't have trapped me, and I can't return there now.

Are you back? Bird is looking at me again. I nod. Bird nods.

People are not different the way they think. We are all shaped by our environment, by the whims of Chance, who governs even Chaos and Night. But people are more alike than they want to admit. They are all Grendel, even though they have branded the first as a monster. When people fight, they hurt themselves and then, angry at being hurt, they want revenge. Against themselves, again. There are too many people is the problem. Sometimes I think I should just eat them.

I look at Bird, who is small like me but even older and more wrinkled than Bigman. *You're too small to eat people. I think you're too small to eat even one person.*

If Bird wants to eat the neighbor adults, I guess that could be alright. Mary is a lot smaller, though, and might be a better meal for Bird. That's unacceptable. *You better not eat my friend Mary, or we'll have to fight.*

Bird throws back their head, the way the seabirds do to swallow fish, and emits a loud cackle that hurts my ears. I clap my hands to my head and wait for the cruel laughter to stop.

I promise not to eat your friend. Bird holds out a hand, and we shake pinkies. A pinkie swear is the most solemn kind of promise, so I relax, knowing Mary is safe.

I'm missing a scale, I tell Bird. *I want to get it back from the fairy queen.*

A wise choice and a foolish one. You would be wise to fetch it back, but foolish to confront the queen now, when you are still so weak. Let yourself grow for a century or two, let the queen become complacent, and you'll have a better chance.

I tell Bird not to see me. If I'm going to be insulted, I will leave. I stand, careful not to scrape the chair. Bird's eyes track my eyes. They see me anyway.

I lash out with my claw, but Bird just slaps it lightly and it crashes into the table. While I'm smoothing the splinters back down into the table's surface, Bird says nothing.

Fine, I agree. *Tell me what I have to do. You'll want something for your help, won't you?*

I want nothing, Bird says. They smile. *I simply miss my friend. There's nobody to talk with. I know I'm old, but the other old ones have mostly withdrawn to themselves.*

I'm nobody's fool. *You could talk to the peacocks. You probably like them better than me anyway, or you wouldn't have left me stuck in the lighthouse.*

Bird laughs again, as painful and upsetting as the last time. *I don't talk with my food. But you haven't touched your tea. Drink up, and we'll plan.*

Chapter Six

The lighthouse is not so far away, as the crow flies, but I am not a crow or even a bird. Bird and I agreed I should find Leviathan. *She's not nearly as scary as she sounds*, Bird assured me. *At least, not here.* They didn't explain that part, but I'm used to people not explaining things.

The mermaids said Leviathan is a he, I mentioned to Bird, and they just snorted.

You can't trust them to know who's a he and who's a she and who's neither. To a mermaid, anyone they dislike is a he. I'll have to ask them about it later.

Supposedly, Leviathan lives in the deep Atlantic, but close enough to come to land when she wants, so it's too far for me to swim. I'll need a boat, and I know just where to find one.

Bigman says he used to have one, before the disaster of finding me, but I don't remember it. And most of the neighbors' boats are too big for one person to use, even if that one person knew how.

So I'm walking to Mary's. I walk forever along the

beach, keeping the ocean to my right. My feet are cut by broken glass, and I can feel the skin of my arms and my head being fried up like fish. When I rub it hard, it peels away like I'm a molting snake.

The sun is almost down, far away to my left, when I see Annea's house. What used to be hers. I'm close to mine. What used to be mine.

Bird said I should hide until night, but they didn't say where. At my beach, I take off my dress and get into the water. The salt of it burns, the wet of it cools. I have a few fish, and my stomach settles down. It didn't like the tea much.

When the sun is fully down, it could be any other night. I could be heading home after swimming the afternoon away and Bigman could be waiting for me to watch movies he picked. But it's not any other night, is it? Everything is ruined by him, and it will never be better.

Up the tower I go, and my window opens out as easily as ever. The chalk has been brushed away, only a little still remaining. With my goggles the little bit that's left faintly glows, but when I peek without them I can't see it at all.

Bigman's ragged breathing says he's asleep already, but it's too loud, too close.

Goldilocks only slept in the bed that was just right, but Bigman is sleeping in *my* bed. It's too small, and his feet hang off the end. His face is turned to the wall, and I can see the rise and fall of his back.

I creep up on him with the thought of killing him. Not to do it, just to see if I could. Nothing stops me this time. I don't do it, though. Why doesn't he understand I only hurt him because he makes me?

He and I are not people who say *love*. Love is not for me. Love is not for him. But isn't that what love is, that you hurt someone only when they deserve it? And sometimes, even when they've earned hurt, you grant them mercy?

More than once, I went to church with Annea, before she was so sad. Everyone wore pretty costumes there, and smiled at mine. Her God drowned everyone in the whole world except Noah for being bad because he loved them, and the people at the church wanted to drown me too to show I loved their God. Bigman said no, and didn't let me go with Annea anymore.

She promised that's not what made her sad. Maybe she only said that because she loved me. Maybe she did.

Even though he's asleep, I tell Bigman not to hear me and not to see me.

I put on some normal boy clothes. *A disguise*, Bird said, *is something that lets people ignore you. If you're dressed as a princess or a dinosaur, people will pay attention. Don't dress as a girl, though.* I put more normal boy clothes into my bag, to keep up the disguise.

Bird warned me *as a little girl alone, you'd be in mortal danger, so better to dress as a regular boy.*

Why, won't a boy be in danger?

Bird didn't answer for a while.

Yes. But it's different. These days.

So tired, but Bigman is sleeping in my bed. I could sleep in his, but what if he woke before I did? I'd be trapped again and we'd have to fight. I don't want either one. I climb back out the window, push it closed, let myself down the tower.

Blackie is waiting for me.

You're leaving for good?

I'm leaving for bad.

She doesn't like that answer, but it's the truth. Bird and I planned all of this, but it's not good.

I walk north along the beach until I come to Mary's beach. Bird's spies were right, that there is a little kayak made just for her.

The knots come open easily, and I paddle out with the ebbing tide.

I hope Mary forgives me for taking her boat.

#

I wish I had brought water. Bird told me to, but I forgot. Everyone knows you can't drink seawater without getting sick, but I've never swum further than I could get back easily. Being in a boat is different, and not better.

Bigman hogging up my bed made me forget some of the things I was supposed to bring. He's always causing problems for me. If he hadn't stolen my scales in the first place, then the fairy wouldn't have taken one. This is all his fault. I'm sure he's done other bad things, but I still can't remember everything. When I get my last piece back, I'll know, and I'll punish him for it. It wouldn't be fair to me to punish him now, before I know all the bad he's done.

I know more than he thinks. I've seen the cruel messages he sends to people online. Usually, it's easy to make him not see me, and it's even easier when he's emotional.

He will pay for it all, and I won't even touch him to do it. I'll just keep him from getting water. I need water so badly it hurts.

Just when I'm getting so thirsty I'm about to die, wishing for the ocean to swallow me or the stars to drown me, the moon disappears behind clouds and the sky opens up and pours sweet water on me. I throw my head back and catch the drops on my tongue. I'd fill the boat with water if I could, but it's designed to stay empty, sealed around me.

At first, it kept tipping me over. My extra clothes are stuffed down by my feet, and even though Mary is a little taller than me it's still pretty crowded in here. But I have the hang of it now. It's not so different than swimming. My arms are a lot more tired, but it's easier to just float in this than when swimming. Mostly because when I swim there's the urge to swim to somewhere, to find something new or revisit favorite places.

It's been forever times two since I left home, and at first I was worried about sharks. The ones near the shore are harmless. Even the ones with teeth aren't interested in me. Some are lonely and just want to talk. I hope the sharks in the deeper water aren't mean and hungry.

None have come to talk with me or eat me, though. Even before I got so thirsty, the ocean got quiet and I stopped seeing ships. Since it's dark, I look down into the water, but I don't see the glow of any animals.

I could climb out of the boat, I could dive down and see, but that would just make me thirsty again, and I don't think I could get back into the boat. It's not made that way.

Bigman took me out in a rowboat once, years ago. I don't know why I didn't remember it before. He borrowed a boat from somewhere and we packed lunches and he brought a fishing pole. At first, each of us took one of the oars, but that just had us going in circles, so he grumbled and took both.

It must have been a long time ago. He's too old and weak now. He rowed us out to sea until lunchtime.

How long has it been? I asked him that what he said was a million times, but I've never said anything that many times. The highest I could get when I tried counting to a million was just over eight thousand before it got too boring. When we stopped to eat lunch, I asked him again how long it had been.

Three hours. We're miles from the shore. It should be enough. It was far enough I couldn't see the lighthouse and couldn't hear any of the birds near the shore.

We ate lunch, sandwiches. Sandwiches aren't delicious, but when I'm hungry they're acceptable.

Do you want to go swimming? I remember his face when he asked it. Why didn't I see how sly he was being? Because I didn't see, I shed my clothes and hopped into the water.

While I was swimming he started rowing back toward home, and I swam around the boat. But when I tried to get back into the boat, he slapped at me with the oar, hitting me hard on the arms and aiming for my head.

Now, I think maybe he wanted me to drown, and I regret not killing him before I took Mary's boat. Or maybe I'm remembering wrong, or dreaming. All I know now is that I'm sleepy.

So sleepy.

#

The sun is a fire monster, the destroyer of all happiness, and I was having such a lovely dream before he showed up to ruin it.

In my dream, I went to school with Annea, but she had Mary's face. Not Mary's face now, when she's so small, but the face Mary will have when she's older.

In my dream, the kids were nice, and some of them even told me I was their friend without laughing after.

Bigman thinks my brain is no good, even though he never says that to me. When he's not looking at me, when I tell him to ignore me and he does, I hear what he says to the people in his games.

Bigman knows everyone online is gay or slutty, and he's not afraid to tell them so. Some of the people are gay and slutty and virgins who live with their moms, which sounds like heaven, to have a mom and live with her. If I ask him about it, though, Bigman will know I was eavesdropping.

I did ask him once what it means to be gay.

It means you're a girl who likes girls or a boy who likes boys in a romantic way.

Why would you care whether someone was a boy or a girl? And what if they're not either one. Can nobody love them?

He got angry at that question, the way he gets angry at every question, especially if he's been drinking. He's not a nice person, and he said some very unkind things to me.

Nobody will ever love you like that. You don't need to worry about it.

Like what?

Romantically.

How is that different than just being nice to people and wanting to be their friend and have good things happen to them?

He turned red at that and poured himself another two fingers. Two fingers is what he calls it when he fills up his glass almost to the top.

Sex stuff, he finally said.

Like you and the girls from the computer?

At that, he threw the glass at me, but not before downing its contents.

I know people like that sex stuff, but I don't understand why. Maybe dragons don't have sex. I saw a TV show that there are some kinds of animals that can change whether they're a boy or a girl if they need to make babies, but they don't fall in love. And some of the animals don't even have boys and girls. I think maybe I'm like that. If I meet more dragons, maybe they'll tell me.

Even though he's mean, Bigman likes to tell everyone he's kind and special. *If you knew what that beast is like, you'd murder it, but I give it a place to sleep and food to eat and let it watch the TV and buy it clothes.*

Bigman has nothing now, does he? I don't need his place to sleep or his TV and I gave him more food than he gave me. Bird says lots of people would want to buy me costumes if I let them, *but don't let them.* So I don't need Bigman for anything.

Bigman is useless. He burns like the sun, except he kills the plants instead of giving them energy to live.

Finally finally here are some clouds to keep the burning light away.

It's hard to get out of the boat without tipping it over, but I'm getting better. I'll be a good captain pretty soon. It's not like I have a choice unless I want to starve.

Where are the fish?

I swim forever and ever, far enough away I have

to put my head underwater to see the boat my best friend gave me, and nothing is there.

Come see what I have, little fish!

I dive deep deep down until I can hardly see at all. *Where are you, fish? I'm lonely. Come be my friend.*

But there are no fish who want to be my friend.

It's exhausting to get back into the boat, but not impossible. I manage it while the clouds are just starting to rain down fresh water for me to drink.

It fills my stomach, but that just makes it hurt. Nobody told me you could be so hungry it hurts. Is Bigman going to be okay? I should have left him some fish.

I should have brought some snacks. Bird warned me, just like the water.

Bigman ruined everything being asleep in my bed. I'm barely gone and already he's stealing my things.

I hope he dies.

#

The clouds do their best to help with my hunger and thirst, sending down plenty of water and whipping up waves that might bring fish, but that just makes it hard to keep the boat steady.

The sun has gone down. Near the shore, dusk and darkness can bring other fish out, but this night didn't bring anything to eat.

I'm going to starve to death here, where there should be plenty. The ocean has always provided for me before, and now, when I need it most, it's betraying me. It's been at least a day since I had fish near the beach. I'll probably be dead before morning, and nobody will ever know what happened to me. Maybe Leviathan will eat my body and word will get back to Bird that I died, and it was all their fault. Them and Bigman, for being in my bed. And the fairies, for stealing that bit of me.

I hope Bigman is happy. And the fairies. I hope they're happy too. They always hated me. That's what Oona said.

The pain of hunger is too awful to endure, and I'm not going to let it finish me off. I'd rather drown, if I even can, than starve.

I leave the boat and start swimming down. When I reach the bottom, I'll bury myself. Bigman can look all he wants, but he'll never find my bones. I know, because we never found the boy's bones, either, and he was so close to the shore and gone so quickly.

Some great beast is screaming through the water, but I can't see it or feel where it's coming from. Just the screaming. I know how it's feeling, and I would give what I could to ease its pain. That is the kind of scream that comes of frustration and pain, of earned anger. It is a threat, but only of self-destruction.

When I stop swimming to listen, hoping to pinpoint the source, the noise stops.

When I start swimming, the noise starts again.

It's hiding from me.

I wonder if it would be tasty to eat. Or maybe it would have some food. The noise is all around me, but I still can't see it. Perhaps it's massive, a whole ocean of pain kept at the edge of burning and drowning.

Deeper deeper deeper, and the screaming never stops unless I pause, never gets closer or further. I can't make myself scream back. I'm afraid of what it might say to me.

SHUT UP!

A different voice. When I stop to listen, the screaming stops, but the new voice continues yelling back.

STOP SCREAMING! I WAS ASLEEP, AND YOU WOKE ME!

The voice is coming closer, and the rhythm of heartbeats in my chest quickens. The whole ocean can probably hear the beating.

Whoever woke that new voice is going to regret it.

The water is tumbling me.

There are great teeth, glowing softly with the slime of previous meals. Is this the screamer or the voice that responded?

This wasn't how it was supposed to happen. I am not afraid of bigness. Bigman is so much bigger than me, and he can only beat me when I'm surprised or let my guard down. For him to kill me, rather than just beat me, I'd have to be foolish enough to think he loved me.

This beast in front of me will probably be my end. Will it hurt to be eaten? The fish swim away when they see me eating those of their school, but they don't scream when I bite them. Not the way humans scream at being bitten. At least the awful keening that had been following me has stopped.

STUPID HUMAN. The voice is not satisfied by the new silence. It isn't near anymore, either. It's everywhere, and teeth shut with me inside.

Bird was wrong. Leviathan is not an ally, not a friend. The mermaids were wrong. Leviathan is not a jumped-up whale. It is something other. Other and terrible.

At least my final moments will be interesting. To be honest with myself, I was dreading the boredom of burying myself in the sea floor and waiting to expire.

I hope the movies are wrong about both Heaven and Hell. Boredom is torture, so how much difference would there really be?

Just let me not be.

I only feel a little sorry for myself and for the others, like Blackie, who won't know how my story ended.

Chapter Seven

If Bigman were Geppetto, I would not have come here to rescue him.

The thing's breath is wheezing all around me, sounding like when the jets fly over our lighthouse. We're not near an airport, so it doesn't happen often or I'd make Bigman put some cushions on the roof to stop the sound. The breath of the beast is knocking me over every time I try to stand up on its tongue.

Just go talk with her, Bird had said. *It won't be so bad.*

When I poke the flesh at my feet with my claws, it moves a little, but at least that lets me find a place I can stand up, off to the side.

Around me, the faint glow of the teeth provides enough light to see if I raise my goggles. Following that glow leads me in deeper, and it continues even once the teeth stop.

The smell is awful, but not any worse than Bigman's cooking experiments. There's a reason I mostly cooked for us. Or used to, anyway.

I'm bored! I'm hungry!

A great sigh.

YOU AREN'T GOING TO SHUT UP?

You aren't going to stop yelling?

More sighing, and a grumble like a cruise ship horn with a cold.

Better?

I nod, then realize the eyes are probably on the outside. If people don't know you've said thank you, they'll take back the gift, no matter how small. *Yes, thank you.*

Another grumble, deep and terrible, but it's just my stomach.

Don't see me, I tell my captor, knowing already that they can't. The times when I eat, and I hope there will be a time I eat again in the future, I can feel the food sliding down my throat. If it was still wriggling when I put it in, I can feel it thrash a bit. But I can't see it.

The faint glow along the sides leads me deeper. Or at least further back. It's confusing to talk about when I'm near the bottom of the ocean. Is there deeper to be had? The tongue isn't sinking away. It's more like a gross and spongy carpet than a real tongue.

Why is there a door?

But we know what to do with a door. I knock.

Silence.

Knock knock! Louder this time.

A swift kick does nothing but hurt my foot. The

label from the hardware store is still on the door, but the hinges are on the other side. Sometimes Bigman used to take my door off its hinges. That was before I figured out he had to see me sometimes. If I always tell him not to see me, he gets so angry.

If the hinges were outside and I had a screwdriver I could knock this door over, like the big bad wolf with the house of wood. I guess I'd need a ladder, too. And to not be so hungry.

Knock knock! Rattle rattle! Let me in!

I put my ear against the door. Someone is in there.

Some coward is hiding behind a door inside this yelling monster.

Bigman doesn't like it when I scream, but he's not here to slap me quiet. I scream.

It's not fair that I'm hungry. It's not fair that Bigman took my scales. It's not fair that Oona stole another one.

It's not fair that I'm alone and that Annea never looked at me the same, after.

The whole mess was for her, because she was sad, because she was in love. If she could forgive me her brother's death, which nobody asked for, why couldn't she forgive me doing what she'd said she wanted? Or at least thinking I'd done it.

I scream and I kick the door over and over, rattle its bones until its teeth would likely fall out if it were a child. Or even a dragon the size of one.

The monster says nothing while I rage.

Everything is useless.

I sit down, lean against the door, and let myself cry. Bigman is not here to mock me. Annea is not here to rub my shoulders and tell me it will be all right. Not even Mary is here, to beg for cookies.

The door still has the price tag on its corner. I'm going to starve to death because the monster inside could muster up less than a hundred dollars. The railing in front of me that follows a ramp down is only lightly rusted.

Bird was wrong. It will not be all right. I will die here, in this sham of a whale. This Shamu, lured from home with promises that the violence would stop. Trapped and died of horror.

The bang of the back of my head against the door makes the voices stop for a moment.

It breaks a promise, banging my head. But Bigman is not here to strap on the helmet. Not here to tell me I'll regret it. Because I won't. *Thunk*. The world goes away. *Thunk*. The world stays away.

He doesn't understand how good it feels, for everything to just

shut

up.

#

The next time that finger tries to poke me awake, I am going to bite it off.

At first, the water splashing into my mouth is annoying, but then my body remembers how thirsty I am, and I welcome it greedily.

It stops, and I open my eyes to look for more.

Above me is only light, harsh but artificial. I pull my goggles down to make it hurt less.

Be easy with yourself. The voice is accented but also kind. It's probably a monster. They have the best voices.

Sitting up lets me see better. The monster is just some human, and less important than the glass of water I see them holding. I take it and drink it down. A small sink lets me fill it up again. It's warm but delicious.

The room looks like on TV when they go to construction sites where the big machines are used. Papers make a delightful mess on a desk, and there's a me-sized rolling chair and everything. The monster person is sitting on another chair, one that's bolted to the floor.

They must be lonely for company. You don't need two chairs in a room if you don't ever have visitors. But how would visitors arrive? If they looked away for a while or could be made to not see me, I could rummage through the papers and find out what they're doing here, in the belly of this beast.

The chair keeps going back and forth across the room as the floor tilts, but its arms are padded so they don't make much noise when it bumps into things.

No windows, though.

What are you doing here?

I'm not ready to talk to the monster yet. I keep drinking and drinking water.

I vomit a little, but there's water to wash out my mouth and then drink some more.

Can you hear me, little boy? How did you get here? What are you doing here?

It's obvious they won't leave me alone without some answers, so I look.

A pretty dress, with pictures of the nautilus animal on it. The face says probably a woman.

I can hear you. Are you a woman? I was expecting a monster.

Yes. Big smile.

To monster or to woman?

Let's say I'm a woman. What are you?

I'm a dragon.

Maybe if I establish that early, things will go smoother. Usually, in the movies, people who live underwater are mermaids or mad scientists. And I already know that mermaids don't look like this woman.

For one thing, she has two legs.

I poke one of the legs, and then the other. Metal. Not the springy kind that the runners who don't have regular legs use. They're more like her legs just turned to metal over time.

Why do you have metal legs?

She shrugs. *Why are you a dragon?*

It's just how I am.

Me too.

Did it hurt, when they turned to metal?

She laughs. It's soft and spongy, like bread. It catches me off guard. I have grown so used to brittle and cutting laughter.

How do you know the rest of me didn't turn from metal into flesh?

The water has made me feel a little better, and I get up close to see if her skin shines more than it ought to. *Don't see me*, I tell her.

"I see you, and nothing you can do will stop that," she promises. I keep looking closely at her skin, which doesn't shine like metal but seems to shimmer a little, the way a nautilus can change its color. The big kids in the neighborhood would have so many rude questions for her.

I have questions, too.

What's your name? Maybe if she gives me her name, she'll want to tell me other things, too. Names are magic. Everybody knows this.

If you don't know that, why did you come looking for me?

She's right. I did come looking for her.

You're Leviathan.

She nods. *Once upon a time. It will do, but people call me Lee when I have to be among the humans.*

You aren't human?

A sly smile on her face. It lights her up and makes her beautiful, the way smiles, except the mean ones, always do for everyone. *It depends who gets to decide what that means. But you're here bothering me. Why?*

Part of me was stolen. Bird said you could help me get it back.

She winces, the way Bigman does when I get excited and make too much noise.

What was stolen?

I show her my hands, the place where the scale is missing.

And now she has Sad face. I know that face. It's the one before they leave and you never see them again. What did I do wrong?

Sit. Sit. She waves at me, irritated now, and I sit. The chair keeps rolling back and forth across the room, but tucking my legs up makes it a fun ride, not a way to bruise up my shins.

She bends and touches the wheels, the chair clicks, stops rolling. She leans back in her own chair and looks at me. Still the Sad look.

What will you do when you get that scale back? Do you know what you are? Do you know your name?

I am Dragon. I am Knot.

When she sighs, I want to hurt her, but I keep myself still.

Are you really Leviathan? You seem like a regular person,

even with your metal legs.

She pinches the bridge of her nose. I'm giving her a headache, but I haven't seen any whiskey here to take the edge off.

You can't tell anyone about me.

You can't stop me telling. Look at me, so brave. Everyone has always stopped me telling. Maybe I should tell this time, though. Once I get away, she can't do anything about telling. I have nobody left to lose.

No, I can't. Even if I wanted to spend the energy, I see your protection. Tell me. What did you do to earn a fairy crown?

I touch my head and feel the thin band of metal. It's easy sometimes to pretend it isn't there, except when it cuts into me and causes me pain.

Oona gave it to me. For not killing her, I think.

I don't tell her about the stone from the cats.

Looking down, I see the switches on the wheels. I flip them all, click click click click, and the chair starts rolling around again.

She laughs a little, and smiles.

You've lost more than a scale.

When the chair rolls over to her, I hold onto the desk and show her the empty spot.

You'll see, later. She's still got Sad on her face, but also Kind.

Do you know how to get my scale back, though? Bird said you would.

Go talk to the cats.

But! Bird is going to owe me for this.

I was just there. Bird knows that. Why didn't they just tell me?

She raises her eyebrows. *They don't get along, exactly. If the cats knew Bird sent you, they wouldn't be happy.*

But what can the cats do?

Tell them you want to use the alleyways.

The whole time I've been rolling around, I've been hoping to see something to eat. I'm so hungry. How could she not have heard my stomach roaring? But since she's obviously going to keep being Rude, I have no choice.

Do you have some food? I'm hungry.

She has so much fish, still lively.

I stuff myself, and that makes me so sleepy.

Waking up, I'm on the beach, half floating, half on the sand with the sun setting to the west.

I should have asked her how she wasn't lonely. *Who did she talk to? How did she end up there? How did she lose so much of her name? That seemed almost most important than a scale.*

Somewhere in the ocean, Mary's kayak is all alone, probably still full of some of my clothes.

If I keep losing them at this rate, Bigman is going to be so upset at having to replace them.

Oh. Right. Bigman isn't going to be replacing anything. And I have no idea how a person goes about replacing a broken Bigman.

Chapter Eight

Maybe I'm already famous, and that's why Leviathan knew where the lighthouse is. But it's not home anymore, so it would have been better for her to bring me further south, toward the entrance to the cat place.

I've heard that curiosity killed the cat, but I am no cat. Besides, if Mary is around I can apologize for leaving her boat in the middle of the ocean. If she knows it was me, I mean.

When I get to her house, the downstairs windows are bright, but I don't see Mary through them, only tall people.

I tell the people not to see me.

Up I climb, to the second story. Even though Mary is my best friend, she's only invited me to her house once, and she didn't even show me her room. Bigman says people don't mean to hurt my feelings, but he lies about a lot of things.

Mary's room is easy to find, but her window is locked, and it takes me almost a minute to get it open.

I can hear from her breathing that she's asleep. The door is a little bit open, so I shut it. A night light keeps the room bright enough that I can see and dark enough that it doesn't hurt my eyes. Poor Mary, her light is just a plain white piece of plastic in the shape of a shell.

Bigman says I'm too grown to need one, but it only took a few days of me waking him up when the moon was new and the sky was cloudy and it was too dark to see for him to buy me one. Mine is a green air balloon. One day I'll get in a balloon and fly away.

I don't know if I'll like Kansas, but it would be something new to try. Sometimes it's okay to try new things.

Mary's closet is full of costumes, but they're boring. Mostly dresses that are all the same except for colors. A couple of swimsuits and some thin cotton pants and tops.

Nothing that would be able to climb through the hedges without getting scratched. Maybe her tree-climbing clothes are kept somewhere else.

In a chest of drawers, she has socks and underwear, some picture books, and some jewelry. The jewelry is fake, I can tell. Bigman used to ask me to borrow jewelry from people nearby, and I would go and tell them not to see me, borrow it from their drawers and boxes.

It was all fake, though. Bigman ended up throwing it away. *I'll take care of it, Knot. You don't need to take it back. It's fake, and it would just make them upset they got fooled.*

Between the moonlight and the night light, it's

easy to see the pictures in Mary's books. Most of them are animals missing their claws and teeth, but she's got my favorite, too, with Max and his wild things.

I have to be quiet so the people downstairs don't hear me. Making people not see you is easy, but it's harder to make them not hear you from far away.

Being so quiet means that Mary isn't waking up, though. Even when I put my face next to hers and whisper *Mary, wake up, Mary!* and wave my hand at her, her eyes just scrunch tighter closed.

I put the books back, moving slowly so the drawers don't scrape.

Mary hardly reacts when I pull the covers back and climb into her bed with her, but when the wet fabric of my pants touches her she startles awake. I should have taken them off first. Bigman always says nightgowns, not clothes, are for beds.

Sssh. It's just me, Lucy. I put my hand over her mouth to reassure her.

When she nods, I take my hand away.

Lucy? Why are you here? I have to go to sleep.

I met the Leviathan, and the cat queen, and Bird, and so many people, though. And Bird promises not to kill you and eat you, even though they could. I wish you'd been there.

Go away, Lucy. I don't like bad dreams.

Maybe it's just that I'm so tired from all of my boating, and almost dying, and then being so hungry, and rolling around in the chairs, but now I'm crying.

I'm not a bad dream, am I?

Mary shakes her head at me. *No. You're just part of mine.*

Nevermind, I tell her.

I push back the covers and get out of her bed. Her nightgown is damp, and I can smell that she's wet herself. That's probably why she's embarrassed.

I'll be back, I promise her. Mary's eyes open wide with excitement, and she starts breathing quicker. Much more of that and she'll be crying at me leaving, but I have other things to do.

If she weren't my friend, I wouldn't have stopped by at all.

#

Blackie isn't in any of her usual hiding places, but it's not usual for me to be out so late at night. It's tempting to go back to my tower and see if Bigman is still hogging up my bed, or maybe he's starved to death.

But crossing from Mary's yard to the ruin surrounding the lighthouse reminds me that Bigman poisons everything he touches. I have only gotten free of him, and I am not foolish enough to be recaptured.

The wind coming from the ocean brings with it the smell of mangrove trees. The sound of it through the dead bushes is a reminder of how I found Oona, the first time, when she was trying to trick Mary. My feet carry me toward the fountain.

Not even a trickle of water is coming out now, and so the stone boy is showing his private parts for no reason, daring someone to snatch him up. Probably he's too heavy. Even when the neighbor kids used to come by and throw eggs at the house, they always left the statue alone.

The shelter is empty except for the bags of fertilizer and the few broken tools. I had hoped, but I hadn't really believed.

I creep toward the place Blackie showed me before. Even though there's nobody around, I tell everything, even the bugs, not to see me. Just because the cats helped me before doesn't mean they'll do it again. Bird and I are friends, and if they don't like Bird then maybe they won't like me anymore.

It's so hard to figure out how people feel. Even people who are cats.

The door is shut tight, but it's not locked. Last time I came there had been no door, and it feels personal that they've installed one. When it opens, I'm disappointed but not surprised that the cats aren't waiting for me, to take me to their alleyways.

I can smell them, though. Like the other place, with the door open there is little in the cramped space. Pulling it shut behind me, I walk toward the back wall, waiting for my eyes to adjust, and don't feel anything in front of me.

Blackie?

If I shout, or even talk too loudly, maybe everything will go away and I'll be stuck in a dark cave near the house that used to be Annea's, in the before time.

Even calling out to Blackie, I stay quiet. She'll know it's me by the shuffle of my steps, the scrape of my claws along the earthen wall, now that I've found it.

I close my eyes as I walk, listen to the sound my feet make, the echoes of my claws. It doesn't let me figure out the space. TV shows always make it seem like if you just close your eyes, it makes your other senses sharper. You can walk in the dark and do kung fu.

When I trip over something small and furry, it yowls. That's not Blackie's yowl.

Sorry. Don't see me.

There's a scratch, and light flares from a match.

The cat isn't small, he's big, but he was lying down. Now he stands up, arches his back, and gives a great yawn.

What are you doing here, boy?

I'm not a boy, I'm a dragon. I show him my claws. I show him my teeth.

What's your name, tiny dragon?

Knot. What's yours, grumpy cat?

His laughter sounds like he needs an inhaler.

They call me Tom.

Can you take me to the cat alley, Tom?

Oh, sure. Tom smiles at me. He has fangs of his own. *I just wait around here for folks to come asking for the alley.*

We can go there right now.

Great! I'm ready to go. I forget not to be noisy, but it seems like nobody else is around.

Tom blinks at me for a while with his lambent eyes.

Did you know cats have lambent eyes? I saw it in a show.

His match goes out, and he lights another.

Is that so? Well, as you're a surprise guest, I can't take you straight to the alley, but we can go and visit some friends of mine first, and then I can take you. Okay?

Yes, okay.

Tom bounds away, almost too fast for me to follow. Having longer legs than Blackie lets him move a lot faster, the way most big people can move faster than me. Not Bigman, because he's slow at everything.

I start jogging to keep up with Tom, and soon we're running side by side. He hasn't lit any more matches, but my eyes have adjusted to the dim glow of moss on the walls, to the faint light that all living things give off.

In the dark, Tom's light is red with black streaks, the way some of the worst of the neighbor kids have. He'd probably get along with them, even if they do play rough. Things with the same color tend to get along.

Not too long, and we are at a low door with a push latch, the kind cats can operate without thumbs. He slips through, and I stoop, make my way awkwardly in.

Friends, come and see, Tom sings out. *We have a visitor.*

\#

Five, or maybe six, cats are in the room but wander in and out of a doorway on the other side. A candle burns in a glass near the wall. Tom sits on one of the other cats, who huffs in protest but then settles.

Our new friend Knot wants to go to the cat alley. Tom looks at each of the other cats in turn, and flips his tail.

A striped cat on my left approaches, swats at my hand with its paw. *You know what that means, kid?*

I'm not a kid, I'm a dragon. What's your name, kitten?

It wheezes cat laughter at me. *Oh, fire. I'm Tom.*

The other cats laugh, too.

Tell the truth! The first Tom is patting me on the back as though I'm part of the joke.

Second Tom dips his head, curls his tail into his body. *I'm Tom Noballs.*

Only the cat the first Tom is sitting on doesn't laugh at this. It hasn't said anything.

Any other Toms? It will be confusing, but I can get used to it. Lots of things are confusing. How do they know whether someone is talking to them?

All but one of the cats, the one the first Tom is sitting on, claims to be named Tom.

What's your name? I ask the last one.

Molly Noguts.

Because you're afraid?

She shakes Tom off of her and stalks to me, flows into my lap. Claws sheathed, she puts one paw on each side of my face.

I'm not afraid. You should be, though. You should go. You don't want to go to the cat alley. Even in the candlelight, I can see that she's soft and blue inside. Her breath doesn't smell of death and rot, the way Blackie's always does.

Aww, Molly, don't go spoiling our fun! I didn't see which of the Toms said it, but all of them start buzzing and stretching, flexing claws.

I stand, Molly climbs to my shoulder. *Are you really a dragon?*

I nod.

I hope so, she says.

The Toms start leaping at me, claws and fangs out. *Ouch. Stop that. Ouch. Ouch. Hey!*

I kick at them, but even when I connect and they are flung across the room, they rush right back.

I don't want to hurt you! I warn them.

The candle gets knocked over, and though I worry briefly that this is the part of the movie where the place goes up in fire and we all die over a terrible misunderstanding, the room simply goes dark.

Molly is still on my shoulder, but she's not keeping me from moving, and her claws are still in, so I leave her there.

Even though I can see their shadows and their dark light a bit, it's not enough, not quick enough to keep them from clawing me. The heavy boy clothes are good protection for my legs, but I can feel that my arms are bleeding, and some of the claws are trying for my face.

Stop, I say. *Stop, and I'll leave. I didn't know it was a problem.*

We're just trying to give you what you want. Didn't you know? The cat alley only opens when someone dies.

Did Leviathan know this? Is she another betrayer? If I die, I'll never get my last scale back.

It doesn't have to be you. Molly says it quietly enough that I think none of the others heard it.

I'll find another way, I tell the Toms. *Just let me go.*

Oh ho ho no. That's first Tom.

One of them gets his jaws around my arm, and that hurts a lot more than any of the play that Bigman and I did, even before he told me we had to stop with the knives.

I don't want this. They need to know I don't want this.

I don't want this! Listen to me, before it's too late! I don't want this!

But they keep biting and scratching and hurting me, and it's going to be like it was last time, with Annea.

I don't want to tell you what's about to happen, but here you are, and you'll know it all anyway.

Run away, I warn Molly. She scampers down my back, and I hope she's far away.

I'm going to kill you all, now.

Maybe if they know, they'll back down. We could

still be friends, even though I'd be sore at them a while.

I've still got all my lives, Human. That's not the part you took.

If Tom Noballs had just stayed quiet, I wouldn't have been able to find him.

My hand finds his face. One claw in each of his eyes, my thumb in his throat. I squeeze. I squeeze and I scream. His brains ooze around my claws. I crush his jaw, and scream, and the candle flares into life, and then so do the few pieces of broken furniture, old bits of food. Everything that can burn is on fire. Everything but me.

Tom Noballs' ruined face is forced to look at me through empty eyes sockets, and the limp body coughs nine times. A small black cloud of dust accompanies each cough.

The other Toms are screaming, joining my own scream. They started when their fur burst into flame, but now they scream even more. Mostly their now-hairless bodies smolder instead of burning, but they still scream.

True Death has come for us!

"Yes." I speak it in the language of promises.

Forgive us. We couldn't stop ourselves. We just wanted the scales and the crown.

Like them, I can't stop myself.

I scream and rend and kill, even as tears roll down my face. I only wanted their help.

When the screaming all stops and I sit, broken, alone, Molly comes back in.

I'm so glad I didn't hurt you, I tell her.

You're a monster, she says. Like before. *But look. There's the cat alley. You should go. Go now.*

I go.

#

Sometimes when Bigman watches movies, I tell him not to see me so that I can watch, too. Usually, they're boring movies, full of people fighting or being naked or both, but sometimes police chase the bad guys through dark alleys.

The sun is shining bright, too bright, for this to be a dark alley, though. The street is hard dirt, brown like coffee but not muddy. It's wide enough that our old truck could creep down it without touching the small trees that grow on both sides.

Bright birds flit back and forth across it, calling out to each other. Even with my goggles up, which hurts with the sun being so bright, I can't see them clearly enough to tell what kind they are.

You wanted me?

A kestrel is hovering in front of me, but it's not my friend from the lighthouse.

Why would I want you?

Maybe you want to eat me. Or you could just chase me for a while. I can fly extra slowly if your paws are tired.

You want me to eat you?

If you don't like me, there's no need to be rude. I can ask one of the other kinds of bird, or some of the butterflies, or goldfish.

Ask them what?

To come and give you joy in your journey down the alley.

My crown is pinching my head, not hard enough to hurt but enough that it distracts me from the bird. When I look again, the bird is gone, and the edges of the road have gone all fuzzy.

If the Toms had just let me be, had explained the situation, things wouldn't have turned out like they did. I had thought that was a people problem, that once something requires a death they think that's the end of the conversation, and it's just down to picking who dies.

Now that I know it's something cats do, too, I'm not sure whether Blackie and I can be friends. Has she taken that choice away from someone else?

Not the fish, obviously. I've talked with enough fish to know that they expect to be eaten sooner or later. A fish that dies of old age is just wasting meat.

I've been walking for a while, and I look back to see how far I've come, but it's only darkness behind me. When I try to walk toward the darkness, the pain in my head gets worse, and my feet don't want to move, the same as when Bigman drank my blood.

It doesn't seem dangerous to go forward, so I walk while I think. The sun is too bright, and it's too warm, but I'm not thirsty or hungry, even though I must have been walking for a year at least. How old will I be when I reach the end?

Finally, up ahead, I see a green wall. Someone is standing in front of it, but they're still too fuzzy to make out.

Hello? I'm trying to reach the fairy queen. I'm close enough they can probably hear me, but they don't answer.

Another forever of walking, and here they are. It looked like one someone from far away, but now I can see that it's two people.

A hairy person with a long beard is wearing a suit and smelling of sweat.

I'm a man, he says.

I'm a woman, says the other.

She's a woman, says the man.

She has long hair that smells of flowers and giant breasts that wobble uncomfortably when she breathes. Her dress is wrapped tight around them in a way that makes them seem even bigger.

Shouldn't you be cats? Isn't this the cat alley?

You're not a cat, though, says the woman.

It's because you're not a cat, says the man.

You don't have to repeat what she says, I tell him.

He blinks at me. *I don't know what you're talking about, but there's no need to be so hostile.*

Even if I didn't have somewhere to go, they're too annoying to stay around.

I'm looking for the fairy queen. Can you tell me which way?

Go that way if you're a boy or a man. He points.

Go that way if you're a girl or a woman. She points.

I'm none of those, though. I'm a dragon.

He turns bright red. *You have to be one of those. I don't make the rules of biology.*

Which one gets me to the fairy queen? If all I have to do is pretend, maybe it won't be so bad.

Whichever one is true, the woman says.

But neither is true.

You could be so pretty if you just put on some makeup. She smiles at me and winks at the man. *Isn't that right?*

So pretty I could eat you up. He reaches toward me.

I show him my claws, where some of the dried blood hasn't flaked away yet.

Oh, you're a rough little tiger. You must be a man. He tries to pat me on the head, but I dodge.

I'm not a man, either. I want to go to the fairy queen. Just tell me which way it is.

Whichever way is true, the man says again. His voice is getting angry. *Just pick one. You have to pick one. Look, there's nothing between me and her. You're a man or a woman, there's nothing in between.*

I'm not between, I agree.

Before they can stop me, I start climbing the wall behind them.

You'll change your mind. This is just a phase!

I can't tell who's yelling, but it doesn't matter.

The wall is covered in poison ivy. I know I'll suffer

for touching it, but obnoxious as they were, I believe the people below.

The only way to the fairy queen is by following the truth, so I can't choose either one. I have to keep going.

#

I was wrong about the ivy. Between my scales and the boy clothes, I'm not bothered at all. That gives me confidence to keep climbing even once I can't see the ground.

I've been climbing a thousand times longer than it takes for the lighthouse, and the thing that worries me most is that I'll die of boredom.

Maybe I should head back down. But that's just as long as coming up.

You're getting bored, I can see it.

I look to my left and a lizard perches there smugly.

The osprey fooled me, but this lizard won't. I can't smell it at all, and lizards have their own stink.

Leave me alone. I have to finish climbing.

Climbing what?

I'm going up pretty fast, and I never see it move, but whenever I look to the side the lizard is right there.

The wall.

Are you sure it's a wall?

It dodges, too easily, when I swipe at it. *Of course it's a wall.*

It shrugs. You know how I hate lizard shrugs.

Could be a very tall hedge.

It doesn't look like a hedge.

Another lizard shrug. *You don't look like much yourself, bug eyes.*

I should eat the thing, but I'm not hungry. I'm not even thirsty.

It's not nice to make fun of my goggles.

Is being nice so important? You weren't very nice to the man and the woman.

That's different.

When it shrugs again, I'm ready. I leap and catch it with one hand, then hang onto the vines with the other.

Up close, I can see the lizard is wearing its own little goggles, pale white where mine are blue. The strap is invisible, which would be nice.

Could you put me back in the hedge?

Not until you tell me what I want to know.

And what's that?

Stupid me. Stupid me. I should have thought about it before. What do I want to know?

How do I get to the fairy queen?

I can show you, it says.

Then show me.

Ahh, but you'll have to put me down if I'm going to show you.

You better not be lying, I warn.

I wouldn't lie to a fellow scaled one. Not even to fish. Would you lie to fish?

Yes. But only so I can eat them.

It laughs. *Put me down, and I'll show you the way.*

I open my hand, and it walks, annoying slowly, along my arm and then into the wall.

Except, now I see I hadn't been paying attention. The ivy surface hadn't changed, but there was no wall behind it. There was only the woody stalks of hedge.

I may be small, but I'm a lot bigger than a lizard. Fortunately, the stalks aren't dead, so they shy away from me when pushed rather than breaking. Bigman must not be the gardener here.

My shoes keep catching twigs, which snap off and tear my socks, so I take off both my shoes and my socks and leave them behind.

Maybe when some person, or some cat, knows they can't choose between man and woman they'll notice my shoes sticking from the wall and realize it's not a wall at all.

Wait for me, I call to the lizard.

But I can't see it. I could never smell it, so that's no help at all. You can't trust the word of a lizard.

Sometimes, when the girl and I would go climb trees together, the little boy would race to see if he could reach the top before me. He'd shout in his little boy voice *I win! I'm the fastest!*

That never happened. Even telling myself, I can't shake the memory.

There's been a girl, and now there's Mary, but there was never a little boy. Bigman has always been old. There was never a little boy who climbed trees, and there was never a little boy who went swimming with me.

I keep crawling forward, and the stalks get closer together and thicker, like roots. They tear at my skin, poke at my eyes, and I can feel tears rolling down my cheeks.

It's the hedge that's making me cry. The pain, and maybe some allergy.

I must be a couple of years older already. I stop and count my scales, but I haven't got any new ones. You'd tell me if you saw one, wouldn't you?

I don't want to be here anymore.

Come and get me, Bigman.

I wait, but inside I know he's not coming. I'm truly alone, with not even a lizard for company.

I wait while a sun I can't see doesn't go down, while thirst I don't feel doesn't make me long for water.

I try to get some sleep. Things are always better when I wake up. But my body betrays me again, and I get bored of staring at the thickening roots.

It's hard getting turned around, but going forward was useless. I don't know what I expected from a lizard.

When I find my shoes, they're full of dirt and green leaves but I take them anyway. If I left them, they'd just mislead followers about the hedge. I push my way out, ready to begin the lonely climb up again.

Only, I'm at the base of a monstrous tree. There's no wall. Lifting my goggles, I see other trees in a ring around my tree. Looking up, they're so tall I can't see the sky, only endless bark and branches.

I push my goggles back down.

Chapter Nine

When you're in it, water doesn't smell of anything much. Buildings stink of who lives there, except my room. I keep that free of the bad smells.

These trees smell of everything, the opposite of before. My surprise that the lizard and the other illusions smelled of nothing distracted me from the ivy also smelling of nothing.

The roots of the tree nearest me smell of licorice. Bigman likes the black kind but doesn't let me eat any of it. He's a sloppy eater, and it gets stuck in his teeth. When he smiles, it looks like he's crawled straight from a grave.

In the mangroves, each root is different. Some like to dip themselves in the waves and others burrow into the sand or into muck.

I move from tree to tree. My feet make less noise than usual, even when I'm not paying attention. One of the trees smells like strawberries, one like mushrooms, one like sadness.

These trees can't be normal ones, though. No

animals live among the roots, no bugs nibble on the bark and feast on the leaves. There's nothing to do but choose one, and then climb.

Oona was part of the mushroom stink, and when they show fairy rings on TV it's always mushrooms, so I start up the tree that smells of mushrooms.

The bark is thick and spongy, delicious to climb. My claws sink deeply into the bark, as though they were made for this. The wooden poles near the lighthouse aren't even as good. I climbed those a few times, but the hum of electricity at the top of them made me nervous. Every storm seemed to knock some over, and then Bigman would complain that the world was ending until the power was restored.

Soon I reach the first branch. The other branches spiral away above me, each as thick as the one below it. That's not how normal trees are. In most trees, I can reach to the top branches but they're too slender to support me. The birds know it, and taunt me from them.

These branches are thick, big enough that they invite me to walk along them. The bark still smells of mushrooms and rot, even though the tree is clearly healthy. It's nothing like home. Even new trees rot at home.

One time, Bigman bought a whole set of new trees for us. *You wouldn't believe how much that guy paid for a cloudy night. Maybe it's time we see about fixing this place up so we can sell it.*

The trees died within a month. Without the deep

roots of the older trees, they fell over, and Bigman had to pay more money for people to come cut them up and move them out of the road. He didn't like them mentioned afterward.

My feet carry me forward, deciding for my head they'd rather go out than up. The bark is spongy below me, and I take off my shoes and carry them so I can feel it better. The smell of mushrooms is joined by other kinds of rot, but when I reach the first side branches, see the broad and jagged leaves that hang from them, my nose is overwhelmed by autumn, by the mixture of hanging fruit and fallen leaves.

I lie down, and I'm feeling drowsy and comfortable in a crossing of branches, except that my head hurts. After I reach up to see why, my hand comes away bloody.

Yanking some leaves from the branch and scrubbing doesn't help. The yellows become streaked with red, and blood drips into my mouth. My own blood. A relief that it's not cat's blood.

Even sleepy as I am, there's no rest to be had here. I run back to the trunk and start climbing again, checking each branch.

Each is the same. I checked three times three times three branches, and each is the same. I can see the leaves I used are missing from each. Up cannot be the way.

Like with the hedge, progress is a lie. I climb back down, passing no branches, drops of blood smearing my vision. At the bottom, the roots wither where my blood touches them. How long would it take until they were dead like the trees at our home?

Tree to tree, the roots are afraid, no matter their smell. Sadness is no protection. Strawberries are fragile. All of the fruit-smelling roots run, the way the other kids did, before I stopped trying to make friends with children.

Finally, one tree simply lets my spattered blood dot it. It does not move. I climb, and its bark is sharp enough that I put my shoes on again.

When I reach the first branch, I am not bleeding anymore. I smear it with my palm, and the places where I have touched the bark smoke and blacken. I climb more.

I climb forever, even more forever than the hedge, and I want to check the branches but I have no more blood. In a moment of weakness—that's what I'm supposed to say it was—in a moment of weakness, I consider scratching myself to make more.

But I promised. It doesn't matter that she ran away, what she called me, that she broke the same promise.

I climb and I count, and when I have passed 144 branches, I reach the top.

There is nothing else. None of the other trees are close enough to see. There is only cloud around me.

Having no choice, I leap, and stretch to catch the clouds.

#

I tried to keep my eyes open when I jumped, but I failed. I scrunched them shut tight, so tight that no light could get past my goggles and my eyelids, and waited for a hard splat. The cold weight of death is dragging on me, making me feel like I've sweat out all my blood.

Bigman always told me I'd fall if I climbed out my tower, but I never fell. He lied about the first owner having died that way. I asked Blackie about it, and she said nobody had ever died in the house. Cats can see ghosts, so she would have known.

Maybe if you die in the cat alley, you just return to the regular world. It doesn't seem fair that I got stuck and had no choice but to leap. I'd curse the god Bigman asks to damn things, though I don't think he believes.

I'm going to miss Mary. We didn't really get a chance to play together much, especially for her being my best friend.

You going to just float there forever? The smirk in the question is familiar. I open my eyes, and the kraken is there.

I'm just enjoying the feel of the water. It's his fault I didn't recognize that death wasn't coming for me, that the feeling was water. Seawater and blood are nearly the same.

The boy clothes make it tiring to swim, and I've never liked swimming with clothes, so I struggle out of them and let them sink to the sea bed. It's not that far below me, and the waves are pushing me toward the shore.

Did I die in the cat alley?

The kraken spins itself slowly, taunting me with its silence.

No, it finally ventures. *You passed through the mirror of the world.*

Where is the queen?

Wherever is most important.

It darts away without explaining, so I swim to the beach.

The beach at dawn is deserted, the sun making the mangrove trees cast long shadows not far away.

Maybe because the entrance to the cat alley was so close, the lighthouse is near enough I can see it rising like a finger to the sky. I could fetch the boy clothes, but I'm so tired of them. Since I'm here, I'll sneak out something suitable for meeting the queen. Even if he's still asleep in my bed, Bigman won't see me.

Up the tower I go, the first time in forever. *Don't see me*, I tell the world in case someone is watching. The window opens easily. Bigman isn't here. I can't hear him snoring or smell his foul breath, either.

He's stolen my clothes, though. None of the things in my closet are mine. Has Bigman already moved in some Internet woman? Did he hate me so much?

That's fine. If he doesn't care enough to save my clothes, then he won't care if I take some of what's here.

I rummage through the clothes, telling myself all I see is someone else's trash. But that's not it at all, not even when I do my breathing and pull my goggles up to look for real.

These are not my clothes. They are the dreams I used to have about what my clothes could be, before I gave up hope. If these are my dream clothes, I know just what to wear.

If the world's happiest spiders lived together and spun and dyed their webs for the queen of the spiders, it would look and feel like my dream fabric. The color is white in the way they swear on TV that white is the combination of all colors. When I run it through my hands, it shimmers, showing off even the low reds and high purples Bigman calls me a liar about.

It's hard to feel bad about killing the Toms when this is my reward. It's not a dress and not pants, but something in between and both at once. I dance into it, and it hugs me tight in all the right places without feeling like more than cat whiskers against my skin.

There's a cape, too, and so this must be a dream. Maybe all of the cat alley is a dream and I'm still lying all burned up inside the cat town. I hope not. I don't look forward to waking up there. If that's going to happen, I'm certainly going to wear the cape.

And the boots! Bright yellow, the center of a daisy against the white petals of my garment.

I don't know where the queen will be. I already know the kraken is a liar and always has been. My space, my clothes, my things, are the most important, but the queen is not here.

I'm dressed to demand the return of my scale, though, so it's time to look. I will find Oona's queen and take back what's mine.

#

The door to Bigman's room is open, but he's not there. I search, but he's not anywhere in the house.

Usually, he gets mad if I go in his room, if he notices, but maybe this place will have another bag of my scales. I'm clever enough to notice this isn't the real world. In the real world, I don't have nice clothes.

I move his computer chair to stand on and find the bag again. It's full of silvery scales, but they're only guitar picks. I bump his computer when I'm moving the chair back, and his monitor hums on.

The picture isn't a woman in a bikini, like it usually is. It's hard to figure out what I'm looking at instead.

It's me and Bigman. We're holding hands, and I'm wearing ears from the park.

This is a lie. *This is a lie!* Nobody answers.

We never did this. I begged him so many times to take me, and he never would. This world was supposed to be better, with its rainbow clothes and its pleasant smells, but it's not better.

Even when I unplug his computer, I can still see that picture, that betrayal, in my mind. I shove the monitor, and it falls but doesn't break. *Jump jump jump stomp.*

It's broken, but I know the picture is still there on the computer. I put the devil machine on the chair and roll it to the window, where I throw it out to smash on the ground below.

I will not be tricked!

Angry now, I stalk my way out of the lighthouse and toward where I met Oona.

Blackie! Where are you?

A morning breeze rustles the leaves of the trees. They aren't dead in this place, more evidence that it's not real.

My shouts go unanswered, and I pass the fountain, where a stone swan spits water from its mouth. I wonder how the stone boy feels about that. Glad to be set free, maybe.

When I get to the shed, I go inside and shut the door behind me after checking to be sure I'll be able to get back out.

Nothing.

Hello?

Not even echoes. I hate the kraken's riddling ways. Why couldn't it just tell me where to go?

I've seen the butterflies and smaller creatures, smelled their abundance, but no people yet. Maybe the queen thinks people are more important.

Bird would know, but that's so far away and my legs

are so short and I'm so bored of walking around.

When I get to Mary's house, I still don't see anyone. Nobody answers the door when I knock, but I climb to her window anyway and let myself in.

Are you Lucy or are you Knot?

I turn and slash my claws all in one motion, still angry at the lies in Bigman's room and now startled on top of it. The voice dodges.

Mary? It looks like her, but so many things are lies here. It smells like her too, though.

I missed her with my claws, which is lucky.

I'm Knot, but you can always call me Lucy. That's special for you.

Mary pats the bed next to her, and I sit. It's bouncy, so it takes me a while to settle down. She doesn't say anything about it.

What are you doing here? This isn't the real world, you know. You should be in the real world. I'm looking for the fairy queen.

Look again, she says to me.

Oh.

Did you steal her body? I leap up, ready to fight for Mary. The rules are confusing. If I ruin her body here, will she be okay in the real world?

Mary is fine. You're the one who chose this.

It's like that movie Bigman likes, where the marshmallow man destroys the city. I close my eyes and feel less confused.

I want my scale back. It doesn't belong to you.

Who does it belong to?

It belongs to me! It's mine!

But who are you?

I'm me. I'm Knot.

She's got me so upset I'm rocking back and forth on the bed, but I know if I look it's just going to be confusing again.

Why do you want it?

Because it's mine! I open my eyes and stare at her, angry at this fake Mary. Would it really be so bad to fight her? Mary, my friend, my best friend, would understand me having to get my scale back.

"It's not here," she promises.

Then where is it?

What do you think it will do for you?

It will make me whole. I pull back the sleeve and show her the ugly lines on my skin that mark the piece's absence.

It won't.

You're a liar. You're trying to trick me.

I'll show you where it is, but you're not going to like it.

On that, we agree.

#

I walk with fake Mary out of her house, and follow her through my grounds. We stop at the fountain. She sits.

Is it here?

She pats the edge next to her. *Sit with me. They'll be*

159

here soon.

I sit, and when she looks away I feel the fabric of her dress. It's not as nice as mine. Mine is slippery, and hers is just cotton.

The swan doesn't talk, even when I make faces at it. If she expects me to be patient, she's making a mistake.

You're just stalling. Give me back my scale.

Look, they're here.

I can't see them yet, though something is moving in the distance. The smell reaches me before they do. The stink of certainty and cruelty.

To keep the clothes from getting torn, I'll have to be quick, which means surprising them. When they get close enough, my claws will shred their bellies and rip out their insides. I will show no mercy. I will eat their hearts as trophies. I stand in readiness for their deaths.

Sit down. Now.

Fake Mary is looking at me sternly. A friend wouldn't tell me what to do. She won't fool me. The bully boys come close enough that I can see it's them. They were small when they would torment the girl, and now they're grown men.

I know I can beat them, though. They're soft and weak things. That's what happens when you're big and scary, is you get lazy.

Mary, fake Mary, grabs my arm and pulls me down next to her just as I'm about to jump kick the first one.

My cape flying behind me would have made me look like a superhero.

Knot, just listen.

I said you could call me Lucy.

Are you Lucy?

I shake my head. *I'm Knot.*

So just listen. Like royalty would. Aren't you wearing a crown?

I wait.

The first man stands before us and bows deeply.

"What would you trade for your scale?"

Mary's little girl hand is on me before I even start to get up. I know it's not her, but it's hard to remember the difference between a body and a person.

Answer him truly, Knot.

Nothing! It's mine, it's part of me, there's nothing I would trade it for! You're the one who used to pull her hair and make her cry, and I hope you get eaten by sharks.

He smells sad, like I told him a lie, but it's the truth. The beach doesn't have any dangerous sharks, but I know people travel to places that do. When he walks away, he's limping like Bigman does. If he looks back, it's past the point I can see it.

The next man approaches. His nose is still a little crooked from where I broke it many years ago.

"What would you give to have her back?"

It's an unfair question. There's nothing that would

bring her back. She's gone, and she's not coming back, and if she did come back she wouldn't be my friend anymore anyway. The girl who was my friend might as well be dead.

I wouldn't give anything. It's impossible.

"It's possible."

And because he's speaking in the language of promises, I can't deny it. This man I broke so long ago is breaking me now, and I cannot handle the revenge. It is too cruel and too kind, both at once.

"Anything," I say. I use the language of promises, too. Even though I've been warned. Even with what happens when I do. I can tell the truth about the impossible.

The man nods and walks away. He's wearing the robes that Bigman does to fool the customers, and they drag behind him but don't kick up any dust. This garden is too green for that.

The last man shuffles forward, and I know it's Bigman before I look into his face. He's younger here, only a little aged.

You're the one who drove her away, he says. He doesn't use promises. Not all truth is a promise.

I know. I look away. He wants to meet my eyes, but I can't. I push up my goggles and put my hands over them. *Don't talk to me anymore. You locked me up, and you stole from me.*

I didn't steal from you. You're a mistake.

This isn't the Bigman of dreams. This man would never have taken me to the park. This is the Bigman I know, the false magician. The blood drinker.

I stop myself crying and put my goggles back on. Mary's face says not to do it, but the alien eyes in her face understand I have no choice.

Faster than he can move, I leap. He's expecting my claws, but I sink my fangs into his leg, into his old wound, and taste his fresh delicious blood.

Stop, Knot. Mary's hand pulls me away but doesn't move to aid Bigman.

I'm not a mistake!

He doesn't say anything, but he shakes his head, and he smells like blood and regret.

I sit and calm myself, wipe the blood from my mouth and lick my fingers clean.

You're mine, he finally says. *Your scales aren't yours, they're mine.*

This time, I can smell the lie.

Maybe I should kill him, but this dream world doesn't mean anything. These tricks have delayed me long enough.

Let's go get my scale, I tell the queen. *I'm tired of games.*

Very well. You have a crown so I can neither compel you nor convince you of the best way. We will do it your way.

Good.

But your way is pain.

It always is, I assure her. *Pain and I have almost become friends, at this point.*

Chapter Ten

Walk with me to the sea, she says.

I know the way, and her legs are short. She has to run to keep up with me. Her clothes make an unpleasant noise when they rustle against themselves, and her hair is not smooth and beautiful the way Mary's real hair is. She runs, but she keeps up.

I lead her down to the mangroves, where I kick off my boots and shed my false skin. The water is warm, and I can feel the tide in the waves, like love in the rhythm of a heartbeat.

Knot, I didn't say to get in the water! I'm far enough she thinks she has to shout. I pretend I don't hear her until the third time. *Come back!*

I sing out, telling any nearby fish that I have special presents for them. None come, and I can't smell any. Maybe I don't need to eat anymore. My stomach is fine, and I called from habit, not from hunger.

This is her show to write, maybe. I swim close enough that she knows I can hear without her yelling.

Come in! I motion to her, but she shakes her head.

The water is not for me. Some of my people are welcomed, but I am not.

Nobody here but us dragons, I call back cheerfully. She doesn't know about the kraken, but I discovered young that they're not easy to eat, even if you can catch one.

That's the problem. It's your choice, though. Get eaten, for all I care.

I don't want to be eaten. I'm sure the fish don't mind, but I would.

What could eat me? I'm not afraid of sharks.

We're here to talk to the Leviathan. That's where your scale has gone. She has it.

She's so far away. I needed a boat to talk to her before. All she told me was how to find you.

Mary's hand runs itself through Mary's hair, the thumb lingering on the crown. I touch my own crown, which has never come loose since Oona gave it to me. It's thinner than the queen's, but much prettier.

Knot, things don't work like that here. I don't have the words in your language for this. You have to call the Leviathan, but whatever you met in your world wasn't her.

I let a few waves pass over my head and cradle me in their arms before I answer.

How do I call?

I don't know. I thought you would. That's water magic.

Water magic is blood magic. I learned that from Bigman,

even if I forgot until he tried to bind me with it again.

I draw my claw across my thigh. The cut will heal in time, and I won't be able to tell the scar from the others I earned during the dark times. Bigman made me forget those, too. Maybe he thought he was helping me.

My blood seeps out slowly, testing the water. Finding the ocean to its liking, tendrils of my blood arrow out to the deeps. My leg stops bleeding.

Come and find me! I yell it to the water. The submarine probably can't even get to the shore. It's too shallow here for anything but the smallest of boats. Otherwise, they would have torn out the mangroves to put in docks and parking spaces.

Mary is looking toward the horizon, horror reflected on her face. Maybe she didn't know, or maybe she thought I was too much of a coward. *I'm afraid of nothing!* I scream it at her, but she is still looking past me.

The lightning arrives first. It strikes the lighthouse, the way it often does during storms. The clouds are not far behind, moving as though the lightning were dragging them. Rain, glorious and warm, adds its liquid voice to the screaming sky, and everything is complete.

I confront the queen coiled inside Mary. She cannot lie to me or deny my power in this place. *This is for me. This is what I do. Where is the scale you stole, or I will burn you to a crisp?*

She shakes her head no at me and points past me. As far away as she is, she won't be able to reach me in time if this is a trick. I look.

The water is running from the beach and pulling me with it. The snide kraken, caught eavesdropping, is stranded on the sand. The force of the water should frighten me, but I can hear the melody of the power drawing it back.

It's singing the song I've heard my whole life in my head.

A head pokes through the clouds, coming from above. What I thought was the blur of the approaching storm was the blur of a neck.

"Hello, child," she says. "You've got some of my things."

#

So what that the eyes blinking above me are each as big as my body? Blinking, breathing, speaking are all signs of life. I am unafraid. My limbs are not trembling. My voice is not weak.

I raise my clawed hands to show them off.

Look, here I am missing part of me.

The thing above me laughs, and it is the boom of thunder.

"I am not a Thing, little one. I am your mother, or you are my tumor. It remains to be seen. I am Leviathan."

I met Leviathan in the real world. She was kind to me and had metal legs and did not try to threaten me.

I can wait until the thunder passes. Mary's body has hidden behind the mangroves, as though they would stop the great wave contained here.

The lighthouse itself would probably crumble if my mother let it go.

Having a mother is not what I hoped it would be. She speaks with the voice of both thunder and promise, but the love that TV promised me is not to be found. The water running down my face is only rain, not tears of joy or loss. The salty taste on my lips is only seawater.

I am not a tumor.

Then what are you, little mite?

I am Knot. I am Dragon.

"I am Dragon. You compare yourself to me?" She is taller than the clouds, and the waves themselves bow to her.

You were small once, weren't you? Bird told me that Hope gave birth to you, or to your parents, and to all of the old ones. Being big doesn't make you great. Being old doesn't make you more important. In the real world, you are just a woman with a submarine.

"You should be afraid."

I am not afraid. I can't speak that in the language of promises, but I do not lie. Bigman has made me unafraid, though those lessons still hurt.

The waves push me away from her, the tide coming in like an exhaled breath. They are not giants. They splash against the mangroves and push me back to the beach, but they do not even get close enough to jostle my clothes.

Get dressed. Her voice is no longer thunder.

I put my clothes on, and though they are wet with

rain, the heat of my body dries them quickly. If I can take these back with me, Bigman will be so jealous of the finery. I hope I don't have to go back through the cat alley.

When she steps from the waves, the seafoam clothes her in green, like a cartoon mermaid. The real ones never bother with human dresses, outfitting themselves in sea moss instead.

Come out, Queen, she says. I hear Mary walk to us, but I can't turn away from Leviathan. Leviathan is beautiful as a lightning strike, turning the sand to glass where she walks. A prince could fetch the slipper from each step and set forth looking for his princess and never find her.

Welcome, Leviathan.

Mother laughs, and it is kind and musical. *Oh, stop hiding in your silly costume.*

Mary is a person, not a silly costume, but Mary's head nods, and she stretches herself, grows and shifts until she has taken on Oona's body and face. The angles hurt to look at, even in my blue world. My mind keeps trying to make the form human, though it is not.

Oona?

Yes, Knot. But Oona is just a title. I am not the one you first met.

Oona, the new Oona, bows to my mother, who returns the bow. Neither makes any moves to touch, the way friends might.

I agree to Parley, mother says. *I see she wears a crown, is she under your protection?*

I'm not a girl, I say. If other people want to think it about me, I can't stop them. In all creation, though, my mother should know the truth about me.

But you're not a boy.

I'm not either one, no.

The old ways say you must be one or the other. Her eyes, the brown of seaweed, disapprove. My crown tightens, but I don't need the reminder to know that she's trying to force me. Bigman did the same.

Was Hope a boy or a girl? Was Chance, and Night? Bird is neither. Why must I be?

Surprise ripples through her, leaving a wake of amusement.

Well. Bird has gotten bold in their old age, I see. What other stories did they tell you?

To seek you out. I found you in the real world, where you are small and kind. There, you were kind enough not to name yourself mother.

Come to the Earth Nail, both of you. Things began there. It is only fair that we decide how to move forward there also.

I don't know where the Earth Nail is, but when she starts walking toward the lighthouse and Oona follows, her stride long and easy now, I figure it out and follow.

Is Bigman to be invited? I tremble at the thought and don't ask. My shame feels like cowardice.

#

Bird is waiting at the table when we enter. Even before I can see them clearly, the smell of blood and feathers is enough to identify them.

We sit at the same table where Bigman sells hope to people with no reason to be desperate. Through the archway is the couch where he drugged and bound me.

Oona smells bitter with disappointment. She didn't want Bird here. Mother does not react. Perhaps she already knew. Perhaps she summoned Bird.

He will be here soon, Bird says. *There was some disagreement.* Laughter, but unkind.

I never met Oona in the real world, so I don't know if there is a difference. Leviathan in the real world had a kind face, one that offered me water, the way a mother would. Here, she is sharper, bloated with anger and lightning. I would not want to be her friend.

Bird is strangest of all. They look exactly as they did before. Sometimes it's hard for me to remember people's faces, but theirs is unmistakable. Their eyes show the same as before, mercy, but the mercy of a clean death, not a temporary escape.

Why aren't you different?

Why haven't you noticed that you are? Bird turns their head to the side, looking at me with only one eye.

What do they mean? I looked at myself when I put on my new clothes. There is nothing about me that is changed. I am the same Knot I have always been.

Mother paces around the room. When she looks away, I tell her not to see me.

Stop that, she says, sharply. *It's rude. None of us are so weak.* Her stride when she rebukes me is unbroken.

I follow her for a while, running to keep up with her quick walk. She doesn't tell me to stop, so it must be okay. Her feet strike the same spots each time. How long would it take her to wear holes in the stone floor?

Because I am waiting for the door to open and admit the one we are waiting for, Bigman surprises me when he stumbles down the stairs. He smells of whiskey, fear, and anger.

He is still bleeding from when I bit him earlier, and he leaves a trail of wet blood behind him. In the real world, it was never this bad, never more than a complaint and pink-tinged towels. He sits.

You had no right to call me here, he says, but he doesn't look at anyone when he says it. Nobody responds.

Mother sits, across the table from Bigman. I sit between them, facing Oona and Bird. We are the five corners of a pentagon. Bigman always told people there was power in such shapes.

"You brought this on yourself," mother promises. I don't know whether she is talking to me or to Bigman.

Knot, please bring the cup and the knife, Bird asks.

I could pretend not to know, but I do know. The surprise is that Bird knows. How could Bird have known and not rescued me? Each of them has betrayed me in their own way.

Bigman's ridiculous athame and his chalice are where he usually keeps them, in the kitchen with the other dishes. Both are heavier than I remember, but I bring them out and set them on the table.

This is everyone who matters, Oona says. She's wrong.

Where is Blackie? Where is the kestrel, and the lizard? The mermaids? The cat queen? There are so many important people and animals you have left out.

The others look at me, and I smell surprise from them all. Even from mother.

This is not how we do things, mother says. *Be quiet, and do not speak.*

Or what? I didn't mean to ask it, but I don't ever like being told to shut up. Nobody answers me.

Oona nods at Bigman, and he wipes some blood from his leg onto the knife and drips it into the chalice. Bird cuts a feather from her cloak and drops it in. Oona uses the knife to cut a lock of her hair. Mother spits onto the knife and uses it to stir the contents.

The four of them are all looking at me, and they seem to think I know what happens next. I peer into the cup and see not blood and feather and hair and spit but simply something dark. It smells sweet, like melted ice cream. Maybe the sweetness is my test.

We're waiting, Knot. Bird looks at me.

You know what to do, mother says. *Do not try our patience. You would not be here at all if it were up to me.*

I grab the knife because all the others did. I take the chalice and drink. The liquid is thicker than I thought, and it tries to resist being swallowed.

Don't resist me, I tell it. I'm angry that I have to drink this gross stuff, and now it's harder than it's supposed to be? All of my nerves feel alight, and my hair is standing on end.

The liquid bursts into flame, and I swallow the fire. It's powerless against me. The taste is overwhelmingly sweet, like drinking forbidden honey.

The others are looking at me in horror, reaching toward me as though to stop me, but they are moving so slowly. I back away from their grasping hands.

The cup is empty, burned clean by the fire. I set the knife in the cup and put them both on the ground.

Don't see me, I say to the others. I did something wrong, and I don't want them to see my shame.

I run.

You were supposed to choose, I hear them yelling after me, all at once, all too much.

They cannot catch me now.

#

My feet carry me south. It's been a long time since this run was a habit, but there was a time in my life I came this way every day, until Annea moved away and left only a house robbed of life.

This was supposed to be a better world, a dream world, but being higher doesn't mean being better. If this is a dream, the girl will be waiting for me. Maybe she can protect me from the others. They must be chasing me by now.

Don't see me. Don't hear me. Maybe it will slow them down just a little.

I am running fast enough that my cape is streaming out behind me. It makes a pleasant flapping sound, small murmurs of joy at the wind that I am creating with my motion.

When I reach the door of the girl's house, I don't knock. I never used to knock because friends don't have to. If the intruders are here, the ones who came later, then they'll have locked it anyway. But it's not locked very well. A little jiggle and telling it to *open up* does the trick.

Rush past *the other door.* Nobody ever opens that, not from either side. The floor in front of it is dry. There was never seawater leaking from inside, though my memories sometimes lie to me about that part.

Her door opens, but the furniture is all wrong. This is not her bed. I throw the mattress off of it to check for sure. The frame is not scratched with our initials. It is not even the right shape.

These are not her pillows. They were never part of a pillow fight. You can tell the pillows that have been because they smell of laughter.

None of this is hers.

I go to the other door and break the rules. I open it, and everything is wrong. Wrong in the wrong way. There are no hastily discarded clothes moldering on the floor, left since they were shed for a final swim. No toys wait to attack uncareful feet. It is only another bedroom. The sheets are pulled flat. The bed is made.

The others tromp up the stairs, showing no respect for my loss, and crowd themselves through the forbidden doorway.

You weren't supposed to drink it, mother says.

When Bigman made it before, he had me drink it.

She looks at Bigman. Her guard is down, and she smells of surprise and anger.

You performed blood magic on it? You acknowledged its autonomy?

Things are different there. You're as much a shadow there as I am here. Knot was getting out of hand.

Bird is laughing at the two of them, though they don't notice. Bird winks at me. Maybe this won't be terrible if my friend is not worried.

The child is mine to deal with. You are lucky, John, that I didn't find out at the time.

Bigman whines, like he does sometimes when he loses his video games. *I don't have much sway with the avatar. You know it's different with mortals. I shouldn't be split like this.*

They're forgetting why I came, but I haven't. *I don't care about your arguments. Just give me back my scale.*

Tell me then, which one is yours? Mother splits her clothing open and shows me her chest. The ripple of scales is broken in the center, pale and red-patterned, like my own ugliness. But she is not ugly. The red lines are not wounds. They are lightning strikes, tree branches, the wandering of rivers.

She wants me to feel shame at being her child. I have heard how Bigman speaks of me, the violence he blames on me. She may be Dragon, rather than an old man, but her love is no less painful. It tears me apart at my seams in the same way.

"That one," I promise, and touch it with my claw. This time she hears Bird laughing.

Oona steps forward. Though she doesn't actually touch Mother, she makes the motion.

The child has a Claim. The way she says claim marks it as magic.

Bird speaks quietly to her, but my hearing is sharp.

You all but abandoned the middle world. What did you think would happen?

I am one of the oldest among us. It was one scale! A nothing! If it weren't for this, she waves in disgust at Bigman, *manchild, we would not be here now. I should gut him for it.*

Her words are an angry threat but she smells of weariness. If she were the sea, the tide would stop in exhaustion.

Oona looks down at me. *Do you repeat the Claim?*

Yes.

You have to swear it.

"Yes," I swear.

She nods. "The parley is ended, and the terms are agreed."

Mother gives a hard slash at Bigman, and his head falls off. It rolls across the floor to Bird's feet. Bird leans over, snatches it up in their beak, and swallows it whole.

Mortals are always a messy business up here. Don't worry. He's as good as ever in the middle world.

I should have found out more about the terms.

Chapter Eleven

Bird takes their claws in mine.

Come with me. It's time to go.

I pull away. *Go to where?*

Down.

If I'd known that, I wouldn't have spent so much time climbing. I wouldn't have sought out the cat alley, and the poor Toms would still be okay. I hope Molly will forgive me for it, even though she called me a monster.

I don't want to do any more climbing. Bigman hates it when I plant my feet because even he has trouble dragging me. And Bird is a lot smaller.

Don't worry. We'll be flying. Am I not Bird? Are you not Dragon?

I am, I agree. *But what am I supposed to do?*

You're supposed to prove it. That's the claim.

Can't you all see I'm a dragon?

Bird clucks. *Not a dragon. Dragon. You claimed the right to the title when you asserted your right to the scale.*

I only said that because it's mine! You can't just let

people take your things. Since you, my first scale, every new one has clearly been part of me. It's not my fault that mother doesn't want to share. It's not my fault that Bigman tried to keep them from me.

Yes, that. Bird laughs, but I can smell that it's not at my expense. *The Ancients, who some call the Powers, aren't the same as the mortals. Remember I told you that I am Bird, and all birds are one? There is only one Dragon, as well.*

I'm too small to be the only one. I don't want to be alone forever. If I overthrow my mother, how could she love me? How could she kiss my wounds and make them better, the way mothers do on TV?

Size has many dimensions. You see me as I am in the dimensions you can see. In older times, people saw me as the Roc, with wings that spanned mountains.

Aren't you upset at being so much less?

While we've talked, Bird has led me down stairs of the house, back across the grounds, and into the lighthouse again.

They give a vulturous shrug. *I am not less. An infinitude of dimensions cannot contain my measure.*

So if there can be only one of anything

Only one of any Ancient, Bird interrupts.

Only one of any Ancient, then how are you and Dragon not the same? Didn't you say Hope was the beginning of it all? How is there more than Hope?

There is more than one Dragon right now because the

dimensions grow differently. They slip apart from each other, and sometimes they collapse or spring into life. At the highest dimension, we are all the same.

How high is that?

I don't know.

So you're just guessing?

Bird laughs. *You can call it what you want. Maybe we're wrong. Just know that things change, and things are strange. Small as you are, not just your body, you'll find it hard to travel beyond three dimensions.*

What happens next? I might have seen this movie. *We're going to Hell, aren't we?*

Bird cackles, and I smell fresh blood. *You've learned such odd things. Down there isn't better or worse than up here or in the middle. But it's different. You'll be different.*

You're not different.

They don't say anything, but they open the window to my room, reach out a claw, and scoop dripping light from the sun, which doesn't seem to mind. *We'll want some light.*

They daub some onto my claws, which begin to shine.

How am I different, then?

Tcch. That would break the rules to say. But you were enough here to force a tie.

A tie? What happens if I lose?

Leviathan will take your scales. Yes, even the one you've kept hidden from the mortal. And probably eat you, though that's not a given.

Will anyone ever challenge you?

Bird turns their head away, looking at me with a side eye. *Of course. But I prefer to groom my challengers and then cede the title. It is the way of Birds.*

Is it the kestrel? Or a condor? Or maybe an albatross? Did you know the albatross can glide for days without landing?

The most promising right now is a hummingbird.

What? But they're puny. I bet they wouldn't even make a full bite if I could catch one.

You're still not understanding about size.

Without warning, Bird heaves me from the window and leaps after.

I don't have wings, but that doesn't stop me from arrowing for the sea. If we're going to fly down, it must be through the water.

I see you know the way! Bird screams it after me. I see in their motion that they could easily overtake me but let me lead anyway.

We fly forever, until the sun sets and the moon rises in its place, and then I dive.

I hate the water part, I hear Bird mutter behind me.

Not me. I'm home, at least for a while.

#

The smell of something close to panic is following me, growing steadily stronger as I descend through the water. The light from my hands means the water isn't dark, the way it usually is this deep.

I look back, and Bird has fallen further behind. The look in their eye is not that of my friend the predator, but that of prey knowing the hunt is almost ended.

I fly back to them.

Are you okay? I stroke their arm, but tenderly. I remember what those jaws can do to bone.

Bird looks to the left and then the right, taking me in with each eye. *I am so old, I sometimes forget things. Your mother is wrong to try and hold on forever.*

I shrug. The feeling of it underwater makes me giggle, so I shrug a few more times. *I forget lots of things. It's usually better that way. When I remember, it hurts a lot. But don't worry about swimming. Penguins are birds, too, and excellent swimmers. Just follow me.*

And you truly don't see that you're more? I'm not sure Bird meant me to hear that question, so I don't answer. When you answer questions people didn't mean to ask, it makes them upset.

We swim for a long time. Maybe it feels like forever to Bird, but I know that if this is forever, it's also heaven. And it's not that.

The ocean is winking light around me, but things are too far away to see what they are. Maybe it's Fish. If so, I bet he—Fish must be a he—probably hates me for eating so many of him.

Are the mermaids here?

Another thousand heartbeats of swimming before Bird answers me.

I don't think so. Sea creatures are funny things that way.

But mother is a sea creature, isn't she?

Not in the same way. She's still big in this dimension, but in the old times she was so vast in the middle world that she could pull a city beneath the waves.

Like Atlantis?

Yes. But I don't recommend asking about it. She gets grumpy.

I laugh at the thought of mother grumpy. Was she in a good mood when I met her? If so, it makes Bigman's grumpiness seem like a sneeze.

I hope she doesn't try to hurt me.

Can she try to stop my Claim?

Yes, and she will. But she can't just kill you or anything like that. She can only convince others that she deserves to keep being Dragon.

What is it like, down there?

The lower world is more definite. Your middle world is made of rules, but they can be broken without consequence so long as one is powerful. In the upper world, rules are fluid. Word binds, but in exact ways.

If there's a place where people have to do what they say, no tricks, then maybe it will be even better than being at home when Bigman is in a good mood.

Maybe people won't lie. They won't say *It wasn't your fault* if they don't mean it.

A few more times, I can smell the worry on Bird, who sometimes forgets they're a penguin and can hold their breath forever if they need. But we talk about the middle world, and the worry fades.

You knew I was near you my whole life?

Bird swims ahead, taking the lead. If they answer, I don't know it.

Putting on a burst of speed, I catch up. For a while, we race. I am much faster. When Bird smells of effort, I can go faster still.

I'm an old fool to try and outrace a dragon in water.

But that's not what I asked.

I didn't know you were near me. I knew something was. Your Bigman did a lot of things he shouldn't have.

But after the boy, when we were on the TV, did you know then?

Knot, I don't watch TV.

Such a strange beast. How could anyone get by without TV? But it's been a couple of days since I watched, and I'm not feeling hungry for it. Maybe it's like food.

The floor of the ocean is clean, the patterns of the waves showing clearly in sand but no life at all. I saw on a show that some sand is from rocks and some sand is from animal bones. This must be the rocks kind.

Do we dig?

Bird shakes their head at me. *That would just irritate It. Irritate what?*

Bird moves away, and I follow.

Below us, sand is lined up like the sunbeams in a drawing. The lines become closer together and then they stop.

A galaxy is close enough to touch. I reach for it, but Bird stops me.

Not there.

We move across the galaxy, too fast to keep track of all of its nebulae, its black holes and dwarf stars.

Night. The galaxy ends, and Bird moves down.

I follow, down past the galaxy, which I see now was just a ribbon of light, brown like grilled fish.

Bird moves down and down and never looks back.

I fly ahead and turn to face them.

The galaxy is above us now, a perfect circle.

A vast lid closes in a blink over the circle, and the world is different.

#

The pressure in my ears tells me we're moving up to shallower water, even though we've kept on in a straight line.

When they go diving on TV, they have to worry about how deep they go, and the bends, and other stuff they make up to explain why they're scared. I can feel a little difference in my ears when I go really deep, but it's like being cold. You just have to decide not to let it bother you.

Are we coming back to my world?

I still haven't seen any fish, but the spot around Leviathan in my world was empty too, so I don't know if that means anything.

We went straight through to the lower world.

Where'd the middle world go?

The part where we passed through the pupil.

That wasn't big enough.

You're still not understanding about size, Bird tells me again.

Maybe if they'd explain it in a sensible way, I would. When I go back home—if I go back home, I guess—maybe there will be a TV show about size.

Surely we can't all live inside that thin sliver of color.

It's probably a year we've been swimming up, and I still can't see the surface.

I look back, but the galaxies are too far away to see now. When things are big, sometimes it doesn't matter that they're far away. When it's dark, though, things should glow or be close.

Bird had started smelling a lot happier when we were headed up, but now they smell nervous again.

Penguins, remember?

That's not it. Bird points at something behind me. *We've been noticed.*

Bird shouldn't be worried. They're one of the Ancients, after all. It's just a bit of glow in the distance.

Moving faster than he has any right to, Kraken is next to us. He's a lot bigger here. His eye is as big as me and Bird.

Leave us alone, Kraken, I say to him.

He pokes at me with one of his tentacles, and I swipe back with my claws. Not hard enough to hurt him, but I don't like being touched.

And who are you supposed to be, little plankton?

Bird squawks indignantly. *Don't be insulting. You know who I am.*

We're still swimming up, but Kraken is easily keeping pace, so his eye stays level with me. He changes to a greener color, like he's laughing at us.

I know you, Bird, even though you don't belong here. But this one? What's your name?

Knot, I tell him. *I'm here to claim my place as Dragon.*

My claws are still glowing, but Kraken releases an inky cloud that makes them hard to see. I can feel him circling us in the water, like Blackie chasing a laser pointer.

Big claim, he finally says. *Do you want me to support you? Leviathan can be a bother, and she's so old. No offense, Bird.*

How come you're so big? You're just tiny in my world. I ask him.

Because here I eat impertinent runts.

The pattern of colors on his skin, slowly shifting from reds up through the rainbow all the way to purple, says he's making a joke.

Would you really support me?

Maybe that was a joke, too. Even though Bird explained it to me a little, I don't really understand what I'm supposed to be doing here.

I'm not sure, he says after a while. *She and I have been friends a long time, even for our kind.*

He doesn't seem as clever here as his small self in my world. Maybe because his thoughts have to travel so much farther between brain and mouth.

But if I'm Dragon, doesn't that mean you're friends with me, too?

Bird is watching me with interest, though they keep swimming up. If they weren't, I'd probably forget and just hang out here. It's not as nice as my coast with its tasty fish, but it's not so bad.

Could be, he admits. *Tell me, though. Have you ever eaten one of my kind? A squid, an octopus, a cuttlefish even?*

Sometimes. They're tasty, but smart enough I have to hunt them.

If Bird was wrong about the way things are down here, maybe he'll eat me fast enough it won't hurt. I'd dealt with getting octopus suckers stuck on me, and I didn't like it.

They weren't as bad as jellyfish. I tried being nice a few times, but jellyfish always seemed angry. They didn't taste good either. Even Bigman's cooking was better.

Oh, you could be great fun, Kraken says. *I think I'll float this one out, though.*

We still can't see the surface, and it can't hurt to ask for a favor. Who knows if we'll have to swim a whole year to get out? I could swim that long, but I worry about Bird.

Can you give us a ride?

The air is charged with his laughter. He wraps a tentacle around me, and another around Bird, and suddenly we're moving up really fast. Maybe I could swim this fast if I wasn't waiting for Bird. I look to see if they're having as much fun as me.

I grin at them, but they scowl.

I'm going to need a minute, Knot. You should have asked me first.

Bird is my friend. Maybe my best friend. They'll thank me when we reach the surface.

#

Kraken takes us near the surface but won't take us all the way.

I could do it, he says, *I just don't want to. You're close enough.*

He smells like a liar, but I don't know which part. Maybe there is some Captain Nemo here he needs to fight, or avoid.

He lets us go, and we swim up, the water brighter and brighter around us.

I breach the surface, almost with regret. The silent ocean eased a tightness I didn't realize I had in me. The real world is bright and noisy and smelly in so many ways. The intensity of it hurts.

Maybe I'm not strong enough to be Dragon, if I can't even handle the regular world. It seems so easy for Bigman and for the people who come to beg favors of him.

Or maybe not. If It were easy, who would ask something of Bigman?

The sun is low on the western horizon, probably only an hour from setting.

I swim toward it, and Bird flies. Sometime in our swim, they grew to look more like a typical bird. A large one for the real world. Not as tall as an ostrich, but full like an owl.

You're beautiful here, I call up to them. *Is this your true form?*

They don't answer, and I can ask again later.

We move west for hours. The sun rises as we progress, the night having taken no time at all. Our swim doesn't feel fast enough to outpace the sun, but it must be so.

Land, finally. The movement of the sun has been more unnerving than anything else here. After Kraken, we haven't seen anything or anyone but sea, sky, and sun.

From the sun it is only a few hours past noon.

The trees look wrong. They are still mangrove trees when we reach the beaches, but their trunks are tilted. They grow straight toward where the sun is now.

I've seen shows where they grow flowers and speed it up. You can watch the flowers swaying back and forth to follow the sun. Heliotropic. That's the word.

But trees don't sway, or at least not much, to look at the sun. A crooked tree grows that way because of the stress of wind or injury, not light.

What's wrong with the trees, Bird? I don't feel any wind.

Bird buffets me with sandy wind as they land.

It's not the trees that are different.

So the sun is wrong? I feel clever for figuring out it, but Bird doesn't congratulate me.

The sun isn't wrong, just different. We're gravitationally locked, like the moon. If such things have meaning here.

So it's always dark on the other side of the world?

Bird nods. *Mostly. The moon is always full. Some visitors from the middle world have called this the land of constant shadows. Since the light never changes, the shadows don't either. Mostly, people have called them crazy when they went back.*

Crazy is one of Bigman's favorite words to call people on his games. He says a lot of awful things when his headset is on. He knows I listen, but he doesn't care.

I can see the spike of the lighthouse. In this sun, it casts only a short shadow.

Do we have to go there? I look at Bird sideways, but that's not how my eyes work so I have to turn to face them. They look at me with one eye.

Yes. Everything centers around the Nail for you.

I want to check the girl's first. Just in case.

From Bird's look, I know they don't think anything will be different, but they follow me south anyway.

I can smell cat here. Is there a Blackie, or is there only Cat?

Bird snorts when I ask. *You're wasting time.*

Are we in a hurry?

Not feeling hungry, it seems like there's no real hurry in this world. When I went fishing at home, it was to keep the hunger away.

How are you feeling? Check with yourself.

I'm feeling captive and ravenous, but not for food. Something here is eating away at my control. It's harder with each step to not simply scream in anger.

I'm not going to be controlled, I say, and take more steps south.

You don't belong here at all, Bird says. *The Nail is the heart of Dragon's claim. Until you resolve it, everything else is going to be harder.*

Then how come you belong? Is there another one of me that belongs?

I belong because I'm Bird. Of all the Ancients, I'm the one who chose the freedom to move.

What did Dragon choose?

She's never shared that secret with me. Maybe she doesn't even know. She's old, but she's not the first of your kind.

I push myself to make it all the way to the girl's house, but the steps become painful.

It's not fair. But it's like Bigman says. *Fair doesn't care.*

I give up and head toward the lighthouse. When I win, I'll go find out.

Chapter Twelve

The door to the lighthouse won't open.

I scale the tower and try to get in my window, but that won't open either.

Even though they're supposed to be my friend, Bird isn't helping at all. Just standing outside the door.

Fine. I knock.

Who is it? Bigman knows very well who it is, just as I know very well who is asking. His voice may be different, muffled by the door, but the taunting and the sneer is something I'm used to. I can almost smell it.

Open up. It's me. I kick the door and rattle the handle again.

You didn't say the magic words, Bigman says, still hiding. *Please open up.*

He knows it's a lie. *Please* has never been a magic word. It has no power to make the bullies stop, doesn't get me the costumes I want. And when I tell people not to see me, it doesn't matter whether I say *please.*

The door opens anyway. If these silly games are Bird's idea of *more definite*, then I'm not sure we're speaking the same language.

Don't see me don't hear me, I tell the world before stepping through. Bird still sees me, but that can't be helped.

Inside, the light is dim. I pull my goggles up to let me see better. They protect me from the light, but they also make it harder to see in the dark. I hope he doesn't hit me with a flash. Sometimes Bigman thinks it's funny to see me twitch. It's not funny.

Where are you? I ask, but mostly to check whether he ignored the part about not hearing. Bird is following close behind. I can hear their breathing and smell the copper of whatever they ate last.

I wasn't hungry swimming in the sea, but I'm ravenous now. Starving, as though I haven't eaten for years. Maybe I haven't.

Bird, if I eat something, will I be stuck here forever?

Bird blinks at me owlishly. *Why would you think that?*

That's what the shows say about eating fairy food. That you'll be stuck. I want to go home after I get my scale back.

No. Those rules aren't for you.

Good.

I open the refrigerator. It's full, but everything is just piled on the shelves without packages or containers. The ridges are filled with blood. Only some of it is dried.

Most of what's on the shelves are hearts. I've never

really liked eating the organs. The hearts especially cook up rubbery and gross. But I'm so hungry that I grab one out. It's bigger than my fist, and I take a bite of it, shaking my head like a dog to tear the flesh away.

I hear Bird shuffling behind me, trying to see. When I move away, they snap up one of the other hearts in their mouth and throw back their head, swallow it whole.

Why am I so hungry?

Bird swallows another heart before answering. *This world is a lot more physical than the upper one. You were gobbling up everything in the ocean, and you didn't notice?*

I didn't eat anything there. There were no fish.

Bird lets out one of their cackles. *You're not paying much attention. You should work on that.*

I finish the heart and wash my hands at the sink. Just in case, I take a big knife and put it in my belt. The clothes have a place like they were made to hold it, just like a real fighter's clothes.

Bigman isn't in the living room, and Bird and I go upstairs to look for him. His computer is still here but instead of the whirring of a fan, it sounds like a small creature breathing.

I get close up and can see that the blinking lights are eyes, their lights blocked out when the thing blinks. It doesn't seem to notice me, but when Bird comes close it yowls in warning.

What is it?

In your world, it would be called a demon.

I thought this wasn't hell?

I didn't say it was a demon, just that it would be called one. It's a computer.

But it's alive. Computers aren't alive at all. Bigman might scream at his and call it names, but it's not a living thing. Its feelings don't get hurt when he's mean.

Everything's alive, Knot. Even rocks have life of a kind. You just ignore that.

Maybe they're right. Now that I know it's just a computer, it's boring. I look for the scales in Bigman's closet, where they were in the real world, but just find his magic box.

I pull it down and open it. Inside, his little knife and his tablecloth sit together on one side. On the other side is his deck of Tarot cards.

I reach for them, but they dart away. In the small box, they don't have room to run, though. It's only a moment before I have them trapped.

The box bellows in and out as the deck breathes.

Dragon? The cards speak as a choir, the sound of many voices joined into one. They sound surprised. *You've come back? Will you rescue us?*

#

I put Bigman's knife in my belt next to the big one from the kitchen, just so he doesn't get any funny ideas about cutting me again. Maybe I should find his mug, too,

200

but it doesn't seem like much use without some way to fill it. Most of the people who came to him just wanted small changes to the weather, the way Mary's parents did. They'd rather the heavens bend to their will than be a little sweaty and go for a swim in the ocean.

Before the boy, I didn't realize there was anything to be afraid of. But there are more important things than him right now.

The tablecloth and cards are easy to carry, though the box of cards squirms a bit when I grab it. *Let us out*, the cards plead. It is Bigman's private deck, not the one he uses to trick people. This one is better, with its princes and princesses.

Bird follows me downstairs, their claws scraping against the floor. Bigman would hate that noise, but to me it is the sound of friendship.

In the really old horror movies, the ones with magic and monsters instead of only screaming and death, there is always some music to let you know the scary parts are coming up. That's the part where the people are going to do something wrong, like making wishes about dead people.

I won't make that mistake. I've made the mistake of wishing about living people, and there's no way to undo that.

The ratty wooden table from *my* lighthouse isn't here in this version. Here, it is stone, too heavy to push aside, but the couches are the same. Maybe the furniture commercials are true about them lasting a lifetime.

The cloth from the box rustles with pleasure when I spread it over the stone. Bird sits and watches me quietly.

The cards are being so noisy that it's useless to tell the world to not see me. When I open the inner box, their excitement is strong enough to smell.

Are you going to let us out? We weren't supposed to be in a box, you know. Only wrapped in cloth. Twenty years we've been locked away like we're nothing. You know we're everything, don't you?

Hush. Let me think, or I'll close you back up.

They settle down, so I take them out of the box.

Before mother sits, I smell her excitement and look up. How did she sneak up on me like that?

When I look at her, she sits across the table from me, but I can smell that she is as startled as I am. Now that I see her, I realize I was hearing her voice. She was saying *don't see me, don't hear me.*

I am stronger than you, I tell her.

You are a theft, an overgrown tumor. You will never be stronger than me.

She's not angry when she says this, but I'm angry when I hear it.

"I am my own person," I promise her. Away in the fishless sea, a storm is gathering. I welcome it, sing to it to come to me. When another storm encroaches, we do battle, and Bird clucks disapprovingly at the thunder of it.

I shuffle the cards, happy now that I spent so long

practicing this. Bigman may be full of trickery, able to put them up his sleeves and pull out the ones that tell the stories he wants heard, but I am the one who has practiced with hands too small. If mother thinks I will be beaten because I am small, she is mistaken.

The thought makes me laugh.

I think I'm understanding about size!

Maybe, Bird agrees.

Our storms arrive, blotting out what little light was flowing into the lighthouse, which is brightest at dawn. The waves surge high enough that they overwhelm the mangroves, push against the shore. For millions or billions of years, the shore has kept the sea contained, and we are weary of it.

There is no secret cave down here, no tunnel from the lighthouse. Still the storm is coming. It picks up the waves, helps them leap the gap between the shore and the lighthouse.

Around and around we chase each other. The windows rattle from our gusting. Soon, the water has crept up to our feet, and my boots are almost getting wet.

I don't care about being the only dragon, I just want my scale. And it would break my heart with happiness to have a mother. I don't say that part. She's made it clear she doesn't accept me as her child, and I won't be made to beg another reluctant parent.

It's my scale. So are the ones on your hands. If you give them back, I'll let you live. Go be a human child and grow old and die while I watch. Your lifetime will be nothing more than a slow afternoon to me.

She has stood up, and she is spreading her arms to make herself enormous. She is filling the hall with her scorn, but it is my storm that is winning.

You're not understanding about size, I tell her.

I finish shuffling and lay the first card.

It is The Magus. I knew it would be. Not because I have cheated the deck. Some of Bigman's tricks remain his, and these cards are too big for my hands. It is The Magus because it has no power to be otherwise.

Don't play with things you don't understand, Knot.

The card has Bigman's voice. When I look, it has his face, too. He climbs out of the frame and stands on the table between mother and me. I do not even try to act surprised.

#

It is not the time for violence. I am telling myself.

But I am still ready.

I have my claws, the big knife, and his small knife. If I strike, I do not think mother will stop me. The smell of her disgust is as strong as the smell of meat and blood from Bigman. He smells like the hearts in the kitchen. Like my breath.

Bigman leaps from the table to the lake forming on the floor. It comes up to his ankles. This is not the old man I know, though he wears the same face. He strides toward the door, kicking up splashes of water as he goes. There is no limp and there is no hiss of pain from his wounds. Perhaps this one is not wounded at all.

Wait, I beg, and he looks at me expectantly but stops. *I'm here for my scale, and I need you.* In my world, those last three words have always been met with scorn. Some of my scars, some covered now by my scales, are from how he made me feel when I tried to call him father.

If I refuse, will you still rescue me?

His question makes no sense. He is not the one held captive. *No*, I tell him. The smell of triumph from mother and his own look of disappointment tell me I've chosen wrong. I always choose wrong.

Okay, fine, I offer. Bigman sits on a chair across from me. Mother shifts in discomfort. She doesn't like how high the water has climbed. I have my boots up on the couch, but she insisted on keeping her feet on the floor. The four of us are on the four sides of the table. I am East, the ocean at my back.

Lay out three cards, he tells me. *These are your past, present, and future. We'll see if I should help you. Just because I am bound to serve does not mean you can compel me to serve well.*

As though I don't know that side of things. But he is being so unfair.

I haven't bound you! If he is going to say such things, I will scratch him until he stops and stab him if he doesn't stop at all.

Are you Dragon? He turns his head to the side, the way my Bigman does to call me stupid.

I am Dragon, I say. *But so is mother. Leviathan. She's the one who bound you, if you are bound.*

If you are Dragon, he spits, *then you did this to me. Here and there, you have bound me. And you blame me for fighting to escape?*

I point at mother. *You did this! Tell him you did this!* She says nothing.

Bird keeps silent, even though they should be helping me. They are *my* friend. My best friend.

Tell me what to do, I ask. *I just want the scale. It's mine mine mine! I don't care about Claiming and whether there is one Dragon or two. I just want what's mine.*

I begin sending the water away, even though mother fights me on that. *I am stronger*, I remind her, and push the water back, down the grounds, down the beach, into the ocean.

You are only letting it do what it wants to, she says. She sneers and stops fighting me.

I am the water and the storm, and it obeys because it longs to be tamed. Bigman told me a story once, when he used to tell me stories, about Xerxes, who whipped the waves for disobeying him. The waves will obey me, even without a whip. I stand and climb the stairs to my tower. Only the soles of my boots are wet.

You have to lay the cards, Bigman calls after me. Later. I will do it later. If I have bound him, then he is not the boss of me.

I can't see far with my regular eyes, but as the storm I can see forever. The water draws away from the shore at my command, leaving the beach exposed, and then the rocky bottom, and then the chasm where the ocean becomes deeper. The wave reaches almost to the sky.

When I let go, I can hear Bird squawk in surprise. The wave comes at us with all the power of the absent moon stored in it. I batter the shores, and the girl's house is swept away, only a few scattered pieces remain. Mary's house falls to scraps. The water slaps at the tower window, but the glass holds.

Even at this distance, I know Kraken disapproves. Let him remain neutral if he can, but I do not forgive.

When I come back downstairs and take my seat again, mother is eying me with begrudging respect.

You still Claim? There is no mockery in her voice.

If that's what I have to do to get my scale back, yes. But I don't want to. Why should there not be Dragon me and Dragon you? Your rules don't make any sense.

They are not my rules. They are just the rules.

But there are lots of birds, and Bird does not demand they claim.

She looks at Bird with a fondness that belongs to me. *I cannot help who I am*, she says. *I am Alone.*

Then why am I here? I smell for her reaction, but she is closed to me. Finally, she sighs.

Because I am old. Maybe you are correct.

She plucks my scale from her skin. When she hands it to me, it is still bloody, and I can see the place where it was on her skin.

My skin is broken and ugly, and I am glad to place this scale with the rest, where it belongs. But her skin is not broken and ugly. The markings on her are beautiful.

You are beautiful, I tell her. She flinches.

I used to be worshiped. They would sacrifice virgins to me. I would carry them to my home, and we would be friends. Eventually, they would get sad, and I would let them leave. Maybe you know something about making friends with sad virgins.

We are both old, Bird says. *Why do you think I have stayed so long, except to keep you company?* They are looking at mother, not at me. But I know the story of the girl who is your friend until she decides you're a monster.

You still have to lay the cards, Bigman insists. *And then we will see what will happen. Perhaps you will unbind me. It is not as bad here, in this world, but I am so tired of being bound as the Fisher King in the world above.*

His body is younger than the body of my Bigman, but his eyes are so old.

#

I've seen Bigman lay the cards enough times that I know how to do it. When I shuffled, I made sure to rotate the halves so that the cards are both upright and reversed.

This place is boring, and now that I have my scale

there is no reason to stay any longer.

How do I leave? I ask Bird.

You have to lay the cards. You started, so you must finish.

Maybe if I just wait here, they'll have to let me go. I'm already hungry again, though. I go get another heart from the kitchen and eat it, but it doesn't help much. The cards are stupid and mean nothing, so I might as well just get it over with.

Fortune-telling is for rubes. Bigman showed me that with his trick of always predicting the same thing. Have I learned his tricks so thoroughly that I'll lay the same thing he does without even trying?

I wash my hands and sit down. The others are waiting for me like they have all the time in the world. They do, I guess.

The card is heavy in my hand. It doesn't want to be flipped over. *Let me keep my secrets,* it must be saying. The sound it makes when I lay it down is not quite a boy's scream.

The Prince of Cups, reversed, Bigman says. *This is your past.*

That's not your business! I yell it at him and run out the door. He has no right to tell my secrets to my mother and my friend. Bigman is the one who taught me it was wrong and shameful. For him to mention it now is even more betrayal than stealing my scales.

My feet don't stop running until I am at the shore,

where the water has returned to a normal level, and I shed my clothes as fast as I can. I hope they're far enough up on the beach that they don't get washed away, but they're not the important thing now.

Bird said this place isn't Hell, so there must be something I can do. The time, with the sun hanging where it has hung since we arrived, is the same, and the ocean is the same, and I know the boy will be crying out for help.

My arms and legs carry me fast as flying to the place where the tide starts pulling out to sea, in front of the ruins of the girl's house. Pieces of wood, broken furniture, bits of fabric, maybe clothes or maybe curtains, are floating around me. On the sandy bottom I can see broken dishes and pieces of the house.

If the storm of my rage broke him again, I will find a deeper world and go there and try another time. Bird told me this is not the bottom, but I don't know where the door is. We entered through the water, so maybe I will need to leave through the sky.

I search for hours, swimming until my arms complain. I switch to using only my legs. The sun will never set, so there is no reason to stop until I find him.

Kraken! I call out to him a hundred times, but he is hiding from me. So far from shore I cannot see the beach when my head is above water or the bottom when it is below, I dive down.

For a while, the only smell is my worry, but when I

ignore that, telling myself not to smell me, I find the boy's scent. It is fresh. It is not too late, the way it was before.

I follow the scent, up and down like waves through the water, but deeper and deeper. And then I find him, the water so dark only the light from my claws, dim enough now I couldn't see it above the water, reveals his form.

I should have worn something to cover myself, but it does not matter now. His eyes are closed, so he will not see me naked.

Carrying a person in water is much harder than swimming alone, but I am strong. I am strong enough. I call on the waves to help me, and they speed us back to shore.

His body doesn't move when I drop it on the sand and put my clothes back on. His chest is not moving when I put my ear to it.

Bigman! I yell loud enough to wake the dead. Except they don't wake.

I've seen enough TV shows to know how to bring back a drowned swimmer. I open his mouth and put mine over it, push the air out hard, and his lungs move up.

Over and over, I take a breath and use it to fill him up. When Bigman arrives, he stands over the boy and me but says nothing.

He watches me breathing for the boy, who is still not helping, still not coughing out water the way they always do on TV.

That was the past, he says. His hand on my shoulder

is gentle enough it could be my Bigman before the boy died. Before I ruined everything.

I hate him, I tell Bigman. Even though I left my goggles in the lighthouse and the light hurts my eyes, I look up at Bigman to make sure he understands.

He nods.

When I look back at the boy's body, it is only a dead mermaid baby. I call the waves, and they take the mermaid's corpse back where it belongs. I get dressed. Bigman is waiting to go back inside.

#

We walk the long way back to the lighthouse. In the fountain, a small person stands where the boy does in my world. Pink-tinged water that smells of blood pours continuously from a pitcher they hold in their small hands.

Wait, stop, I tell Bigman. Something is wrong with this statue. The figure has been broken and rebuilt, and the cracks spider across their arms and legs, everywhere that the clothes don't cover. In the constant light, the cracks seem to be filled with molten gold, and there is a beauty to the pattern that makes me envious but also feels achingly familiar.

I sit down to stare. It would be better if I had my goggles. The statue is almost glowing from the light, and my head is hurting. It was foolish of me to go without them, for nothing. The boy has been dead a long time, and I know magic doesn't work to bring dead things back.

Bigman promises a lot of things to the people who pay him, but he never promises that one.

What did you mean before, about being bound as the Fisher King? I shade my eyes with my hand and look up at him. He frowns but sits next to me on the edge of the fountain. I slip off my boots and put my feet in the water. It is cool, even though I am not hot.

There is a myth, he says, *of a king who lives by the ocean. He's hurt and can only sit and fish. The whole land around him is a wasteland and stays that way until he's healed.*

So everything suffers because he's bad?

I splash my feet around while he thinks. The motion of the water breaks up the reflection of the statue, highlights its cracked image. If only I were as beautiful as this stone creature, people would want me to pour water endlessly out for them.

I stop my feet to get a better look. The glare from the sun is too much to look at the statue directly, but the water is only a little shiny.

The reflection tilts its head, and I look up at the statue, startled. It gazes toward the sea, its neck unbent. Looking back at the reflection, I realize what should have been obvious. It's me. Except I'm beautiful. By reflex, I want to deny it, but Bird was right that things are more definite here.

The final scale must have transformed me. I pull back my sleeves and look at the broken lines that cover them. They're still red, and my skin is still white as good marble, but the lines are those of an artist, not a butcher.

He's not bad, Bigman says. I had forgotten I'd asked him a question. *It's not certain why he's cursed. Because there's no doubt he's cursed.*

What does it mean to be bound?

I know Bigman is bad, so maybe he's not this Fisher King. It would be just like him to invent a story where he's tragic. He thinks I don't see him sometimes, watching sad movies and crying. Feeling sorry for himself, I know.

It's different here than there. Here, it means I can't travel far from the Nail. Unless someone summons me, the way you did, I'm stuck with the others in the deck.

If I unbind you, what happens?

He shrugs at me. I remember him being this young, his back being straight like this, and his beard not being flecked with white. It has been a long time. Maybe this place is what's made both of us more beautiful. Will I lose it when I return?

I don't think you can do it here. Most people are just ideas, but I happen to know what idea I am. The archetype of the magus dates back to the beginning of the world. It might even be older than both of the others. The Fisher King is newer.

So I can let Bigman go, but not you?

He takes off his boots and kicks his feet in the water next to mine. Bigman would never do that, and it reminds me that this one is an impostor. Would be an impostor if he were in my world, I guess. I am the impostor here.

Maybe. You have to get back first. Healing the Fisher King has always required the grail and the right questions.

He already has the grail.

Bigman snorts. *A grail, anyway. It would probably do. The grail is another archetype, no more free than I am.*

The temptation is strong to stay here forever. The sun would never set, and this Bigman has to do what I say, it seems.

But I am so very hungry. I stand in the fountain and drink the water flowing from the pitcher. It tastes of blood, like everything here, and only makes my hunger worse.

I dry my feet and put the boots back on. I'll lay the cards if that's what it takes to escape before I starve. But first, there's a refrigerator calling my name.

Chapter Thirteen

Three hearts is barely enough to make me feel anything other than hunger again. I think they're getting smaller. Bird probably ate all of the big ones. They seem like the selfish type, especially here.

I wash the blood off my hands and go sit. Put my goggles back over my eyes to make the burning stop. Bird and mother were talking too quietly for me to hear, and with Bird there I can't even hide and listen.

Bigman settles himself across from me, an expectant look on his face.

You already know what's next, don't you? I ask him.

He gives me a smile. Sly, but not amused. *You do, too,* he says.

The first time I saw Bigman lay the cards, however many miseries ago, they had seemed to crackle with magic. His hands had danced around the table, and the people were caught up in the spell he was weaving. They gave him cash right then, and he made a note in his book about what they wanted.

Over too many forgotten times, when all the people got the same cards, the magic was shown to be no more real than ghosts, who were usually just old men hiding themselves in white robes and trying to scare children. Magic or no, Bigman could make the cards dance. He'd only stopped making playing cards dance when that man had pulled a gun and accused him of cheating.

Don't see me, I had told the man and stood at his elbow, watching to see what he would do. Bigman had trembled and started spinning lies, denying he was cheating. Not his fault the other guy had bad luck. *Shoot him*, I whispered to the man. He'd taken all the money and then broken Bigman's nose with his fist. Maybe he didn't hear me, maybe he decided to ignore it.

After that, Bigman carried playing cards only to go do magic at children's parties. This didn't last long. *The parents are too demanding*, he said. *They don't recognize real magic and they pay peanuts.* He hadn't shared the peanuts, nor brought cake.

Knowing how the cards could be faked, that the others had all been here when I went to rescue the boy, I didn't trust them. I peeked at the top card. The princess of cups, the way I knew it would be. In this place, it had Annea's face. She frowned at me. Behind her, a great bird spread its wings, and beside her a great scaled thing swam. Even in pictures, Bird and mother couldn't leave my pain alone.

I shuffled the deck again and again. Touching them after the first shuffle and cut was against the rules, but those rules were meant to let Bigman cheat. If they were truly my future, it wouldn't matter what I did. I was careful to make sure the princess wouldn't be on top. If Bigman or the others saw, they didn't say anything. Cunning can be magic any day.

When I turn the card, the eight of swords shows. *INTERFERENCE* is written on it. I look up at Bigman with shame. Cheating is wrong, and just because he does it doesn't mean I should.

Are you really surprised? he says.

I put it back and shuffle the deck, not cheating this time, and then turn the card. It's the princess, of course. She's older. Happier. Because she's far from me.

This is your present, Bigman says.

But she's not my present. She's my past! She called me a monster and left me! There's nothing present about her.

Bird clears their throat. It's probably so noisy because of how piggy they were with the hearts. They croak out their question. *Do you think about anything else?*

Yes, I say. *I think about being trapped, and being hungry, and how none of this is my fault. It was Bigman who made me do it. He told me she would be happier if I did. He LIED to me!*

\#

Come talk with me, Annea's voice promises me from upstairs. My feet carry me that way without hesitation, despite my spirit's desire to flee, and I don't know which of them is the traitor.

She's lurking in the library, splayed like a broken thing on the desk, all flat and photographed in the album of hurts. Here she is as I remember her the first day, next to me in a black-and-white photo we never took, both of us dressed to swim in costumes we never wore.

I have not aged a day or a year or a decade since that time, but she has moved backward and become a child again. Young enough to not have learned lessons she should never have known. I was her worst teacher.

"You're in the past," I promise her picture. No magic should be needed to make it so. There is no truth in which it is not that way. If ghosts were real, hers would not be one to haunt me. She still lives, in some other world.

Things only remain in the past if you stop digging them up, she says to me. Her voice is not a child's voice. It is the voice that revoked her wish, uselessly, when it was too late to undo things.

The feel of blood congealing in my stomach is stuffing up my eyes until my blinking sends tears down my face to puddle in my goggles. When I dump them, it is blood splashing on the pictures. Everything here is blood. Why did I gorge myself on it when I could have just breathed it in?

Her swimsuit dapples from gray to red, her cheeks flush with color, and her voice, all of her voices, whisper scream at me. *Tell me what you did,* she demands.

You already know.

Tell me again. I know only what my eyes saw, not what yours saw. Not what was in you to do. Not why.

If this place were kind, she would be here in body, even if it were only a lurching hunk of meat like in one of the zombie movies. This place is not kind. A picture cannot feel you trying to hug it, can neither accept nor reject.

But I have come too far. Having taken my self, my scale, I must escape this place of relentless hunger and obligation and magic I don't understand.

I drowned your brother, I remind her.

Are you the ocean, then?

At my command, the waters rise, begin to form themselves in another great wave that will crash against the windows of this Nail and remind her of the answer.

And as the waters rise and the power gathers, she laughs at me. Not the way Bigman laughs, but the way she used to laugh when we played in her room with toys Bigman would never grant me.

I am the ocean now, I tell her.

But were you the ocean then?

I want to tell her I was, but it would be a lie. How would Bigman have trapped an entire ocean? His bloody double said it plain: he is trapped as much as I am. He got greedy when he plucked me from the shore, and now he is stuck between powers that could destroy him without noticing they had done so.

"No," I croak.

Did you weep when he died?

She knows I did. She knows I nearly drowned myself, impossible as that seems now, searching for his body.

But you called me monster, I remind her.

Her picture flicks me a paper-cutting glance. *You know that's not why. Say what you did, if you ever want to be free.*

This is not my present! The demon computer snoozing beneath the desk rouses and gives me the evil eye. I don't pluck it out.

The thing you did is your past. This torment you wreak upon yourself is your present. Do I lie?

No, Annea. Never. Never a lie.

What can this memory of her, this flat tormentor do to me if I speak the truth? Break me? As though I have not been broken into shards that Bigman and the others claimed as trophies and used to amuse nobodies by playing guitar badly with my hurts.

I killed your father, too. After your brother drowned.

Tell me how. Tell me the details.

After the boy died, Annea's father had begun to threaten Bigman. He would sue. He would take the lighthouse away. He would have Bigman arrested for negligence. The bellow of his voice in the mornings was more regular than the later mockery of the peacocks.

You have to stop him, Bigman had told me.

How? I had been only ten or a hundred or a thousand

years old, too naive to see the trap.

Climb in his window after night has fallen. Stab him in the heart. Bigman had given me his athame, useless and dull as it was, to perform his ragged task. And once, after many years, Annea had wished him dead. If she hadn't, I would have told Bigman no. I swear I would have.

#

This is supposed to be my present, but I am back in the past now.

I dress in white, a halo above my head, wings drooping from my back. The last time I will ever pose as an angel.

Bigman hasn't told me when to do the magic that will make Annea's father's complaints disappear, but he doesn't need to say it. He always means *now* when it is for me to do, *later* when it is for him to do.

The sky has collapsed into night. Both cloudless and starless. Bigman told me enough times that he refused to explain it further about light pollution. But I know now— the future now, I mean—that even the stars do not want to witness my actions.

I skulk to the edge of the property. If any people are on the beach below, they see an angel drifting through half-rotted plants, the shush of footsteps in sand against concrete revealing the lie told by the wings. I cannot fly. Not yet. Not then.

When I visit Annea for our childish delights, for games and laughter and the illusion that we are friends, I go in through the front door, up the stairs to her sanctum. I am not here for Annea.

Bigman's dull dagger is tucked into a sash at my waist. It does not make any noise as I begin to climb the house. The climb does not take long. The house does not have a spike. Between the railings, the gutters, the decorative plants, I could climb blindfolded.

I have done so sometimes to make Annea clap with amazement. Her once-brother once clapped, too. Neither claps this time. If her brother sees me from Heaven or wherever he is, he says nothing I can hear.

The window opens easily at my touch. Annea's father lies in his bed.

I crawl on top of the bed, curl myself above his face, deciding whether it would be best to stab him in the heart, the throat, the eye. On the TV shows, they usually stab people in the stomach, but those people often recover. They always scream.

In some of the movies, a quick slash across the throat is enough to ensure both silence and a painless end. I take the athame from my sash and run it across my hand. Nothing. Not blood, not even a scratch. I do not have my armored hands yet, it is simply a useless bauble for what Bigman wants.

The man is deep asleep. His breath is silent, and he shows no sign he has noticed me, not even after I forgot to be careful about bouncing the bed.

I slap him once in the face. Not hard. I don't want to make too much noise. But hard enough. When he wakes and sees my knife pointing at his eye, he won't know how useless it is likely to be.

He does not wake. Not even when I slap him a second time. A third. A desperate fourth. Loud enough to wake the others if they are light sleepers. His breath is slow enough I can't see it. I put my ear to his chest, and his heart is so faint even I can barely hear it. It sounds like the echo of my own heartbeat.

It is not supposed to go this way. How can I kill him if he's dead already? Bigman is going to be so angry. What will he do to me when I report my failure?

I drop my knife and straddle him. Stab down with my clenched fists in a rhythm I've seen on so many hospital shows. Four slow, four fast. He is too big, and I am too small, and despite my best magics, despite my most furious need to be the one to kill him, my CPR does not bring him back.

His final breath is not even strong enough to count as a sigh. It is simply an end.

In my frustration, I grab my dagger and jab him hard as I can in the chest. It slides off his ribs, barely rips his pajamas to leave a thin line of blood. But my scream has woken Annea.

She turns on the light. I am blinded, caught with a bloody knife in my hand, a dead body below me.

I run.

No, I fly. My first flight, out the window, a leap from too high but my fear or my wings carry me to the ground with only a sharp jolt in my feet before I'm tumbling and then up again and running back to the lighthouse. Annea's scream of "MONSTER!" lopes after me as I run, clambers up the lighthouse as I climb, falls away when I slam the window shut on it.

My room is empty. I change into my pajamas and creep downstairs.

Bigman waits for me there.

Give me the tool, he demands. I hand it to him, and he jabs his hand, then my own. Three sets of blood on it now. He stirs something in his grail and tells me to drink. I drink.

"I bind you by blood", he says. "Remember it always, that you murdered him. Forget this always, that I bound you."

But nothing is forever. I know it now.

I know what I did. I know what I didn't do. I don't know which is more monstrous.

\#

How many times must Bigman have bound me before I started to forget to forget it? Waking this way feels too familiar. Waking up should not feel like regret, but how much of this time have I been waking into dreams he plotted for me?

My sanguine Annea is quiet in the photo album, and I

reach out my hand, stroke her face tenderly with one of my claws. Somewhere in another world, she might know that I killed neither her brother nor her father.

Do you know I didn't do it? I ask this false copy of her in this low place.

She chooses to remain mute, so I accuse myself for her. *You tried to do it. Failing does not excuse you.*

The others are waiting downstairs. They're here because of me, and since the sun doesn't move in the sky and the ocean moves only at my command, and there are no birds in the sky, only Bird on the furniture, there is no hurry.

I head further upstairs, open my window, and leap out, rather than scaling down. The waves of the ocean will not, cannot, rise fast enough to keep me from shattering against the ground below. Though the moon is immeasurably vast, even She cannot lift a wave fast enough.

I am also an ocean, Sky reminds me, lifts me unkindly and sets me ungently down outside the tower. I refuse to enter.

I walk for what must be a year to get away from this place, and every month I find myself back here both hungry and bloated, angry and inconsolable.

Bigman always tells me I am not the center of the universe, but in this place he would be lying to say so. I can remain in the eternal present. All it costs is the ability to change.

Like the mother who scorns me but has given me back my scale. I have made my claim. Despite remembering that

I did not kill Annea's family, I am still a killer. Not only the fish I killed to fill my belly, the Toms I killed to fill my pride, but also the uncountable futures I have murdered by stubbornness or haste.

Yes oh yes, I am a thing with fangs and claws. So be it.

I rip open the door with all the strength in my arms, stride through it, slam it shut behind me. Each of the others looks back impassively when I glare at them.

That mother and Bird do nothing agrees with what I've known of them since my scale was first stolen, and no new knowledge from the return of it causes me surprise. Bigman should know his peril, though.

"You killed her father before you ever sent me!" I am angry enough to shout promises at Bigman. He opens his mouth. I leap, fly, ride a wave of Sky before he can get out a word, and slash him through the throat.

Mother should be proud, but she only jerks her head back toward Bigman when I look to her.

I am not the one above, he says. His neck is undamaged, his head still atop it.

You've made me angry, I tell him, and slash again and again. I can feel his flesh tearing beneath my claws, which barely catch at the fabric of his robes when my aim is low. I can smell his blood spraying the room, coating us all in this vital elixir. I slash until my arms are tired.

And there he sits, unharmed.

You can't kill an idea by direct violence, mother finally remarks.

My scales itch. I scratch at them while I catch my breath. The newest, the one she handed to me only an eternity ago, falls from me, drifting like an autumn leaf.

Mother's hand shoots out and grabs it. She places it back in the void of its absence. The tiniest of smiles crosses her face, only the echo of gloating.

Bird clears their throat again. *Your Claim is in dispute,* they croak out.

I will not be denied after fighting so hard for what is mine. Already I have started to forget what the scale taught me. But Annea has reminded me: beginnings are not endings.

The athame comes eagerly to my hand. It is dull as ever, awkwardly balanced, too long to be a sword, too short to be concealed by one as small as me.

When I stab Bigman with it, with this idea of a knife, he crumples into the couch, shrinks away until The Magus card is all that remains, its corner slightly dogged.

I pick it up.

You've made a start, he tells me, *be sure to make a finish of keeping your promise.*

Mother's answer is a low growl. *Put it back in the deck. This changes nothing.* She covers our scale with her hand. Her sudden modesty confirms my victory.

The card is the wrong shape. The wrong material. The wrong idea.

I understand, I say to Bird. My friend, who was trying to

teach me even when I rejected them.

I lay The Magus, but not on the table. Not back into the deck. I fit it to the ragged edge of my scales.

I understand about size. The card shimmers, contorts, and becomes part of me. Bigman has always been part of me. Perhaps he is right that I am not his child, but he is my parent. The asymmetry is painful but irrelevant. Does mother know that now I will always be part of her?

I open the door. Oona is standing outside, as I knew she would be.

Come in, I invite her.

She glides in, her face unreadable.

There is no need for any of them to ask. Bigman's knowledge of magic is mine. The rituals must be satisfied.

I turn the final card.

The Tower. It is time for me to return. There is no future in which I don't.

#

When I head for the door, Oona holds up a hand to stop me from leaving.

Sit, little one.

Bird is already sitting. Oona is not much taller than me. Only mother could never be called little one. Oona glares at me, and I sit. I can be gracious in my victory.

The others must know that I know, now, what is expected of me. Not my problem that they are all too scared to take the first steps. I already climbed forever into the sky, swam forever through the ocean, walked forever across the grounds. My patience is an endless war.

Bird clears their throat. Nobody is fooled that the noise was necessary. Mother is glaring at me. Her eyes are stormy, but I keep both Ocean and Sky from speaking. Let her say it first.

She says nothing, so I shrug at her, go to the refrigerator and grab another one of the hearts. It is still dripping a little, but I bring it out and sit anyway. Despite my hunger, my own longing to go back, find the real Bigman, the one who is real to me, I take only small bites. They can make me speak neither by their silence nor by my hunger.

Impossible to say how long we all wait. Bird must have cleared their throat a bazillion times by now, but the silence resists their attempts to break it.

"Have your games," mother finally says. Her admissions unleashes me, releases us from this silly deadly contest that I was always going to win.

I will go back to the upper world, I tell them. *And be Dragon.*

Mother sneers, but her hearts aren't in it. Most of them still wait in the fridge. *Will you slay Leviathan to claim your title?*

Her words make me flinch. Why is she so cruel, even to the self she claims? *Of course not*, I tell her without promising. *She was kind to me, once I found her.*

You know that you cannot be Dragon in that world so long as another holds that title.

I am tired of her lies. The words she says may be true,

but the words she leaves out are also true. *I can be one of a crowd. Not everything has to be alone.*

She bristles and flares her nostrils. *What is not singular is weak.* When she says this, she is moving herself, unable to stop preening at the symmetry and beauty of her scales. They are not singular but myriad.

I shrug. Bigman is another who thinks he's got to be special to be worthwhile, but it's an illusion. Blackie is no less special for being one of the many cats in the cat kingdom. The shows with more than one character are a lot more fun than the ones that stick to a single set of eyes.

Oona, I say and look at her. Nobody cares what mother or Bird have to say. This is between me and Oona now. *I'm ready to leave.*

She nods, but her posture is tense, ready for argument. *Do you understand what you're agreeing to?*

Yes. Maybe. But expressing doubt won't get me out of this place, back to where I can satisfy my hunger by eating, my exhaustion by sleeping, my boredom by swimming in the dark.

Back up is not the only direction I could go. I trace the edge of the Magus card where it has merged with my skin. It does not have the hard strength of the other scales, but it is not weak. It feels more like skin.

From the shows on the TV, I know that nobody would give a tattoo to one as small as me, unless maybe I was in prison where everyone gets one. Bigman has marked me enough times that I know he is willing, but it is not the same. My skin speaks to me now. The scales say only *Danger* and *Keep away!* They scream it to the world. The card speaks to only me. I ask the Magus if I've kept my promise and set him free, but he doesn't answer. Not yet.

I could go inward, toward the center, where things would be different. Where Annea might still love me but wouldn't be herself. She would be part of all the ideas of her. Not even my skin knows whether I would also find myself waiting further inward. Whether mother and I would be the same, whether I could burrow far enough to join with every other thing as Night or Chaos or Hope or whatever the first power was. Whether I would be eaten by something bigger than me and lose the will to move further in.

I will go back up, then, back to the world I claim as mine even when it rejects me. Annea is not dead, after all. Maybe I am dead to her, but there is no symmetry in the world above.

Let's go, I tell Oona. I am impatient. An hour or a million years, however long I have been here has been too long. Maybe I will regret later having yielded the scale so easily.

It is still mine. There will be a day I collect it. That day is not any of the todays.

#

Oona leads me to the edge of the property, toward the place where in my world the cat kingdom has its opening.

We're not using your gate? I ask her.

She is part of me here, but in your world I am her queen. I would no more invite myself into her home here than I would in your world. Only part of me belongs.

A twinge from my crown. She is not telling me the whole truth. As though anyone ever does. But I know the unscratched itch of being in a place you're not wanted.

Bigman thinks he's taken all of my secrets. Or he thought so, anyway. I showed him his error when I escaped, and he was helpless to stop me leaving. He will be equally helpless to stop me returning with his icon a part of my being.

We do not stop at the entrance to the cat kingdom, if such even exists here. Perhaps Cat is only a part of Claws here. The lizard is probably part of mother, the avatar of Scales. I have not seen Blackie in any form since I arrived. Beyond the door is more field and then the trees that begin Bird's domain. We head into those trees.

I have more years of experience with the fairies as they appear on the TV shows, as friendly and maybe a little too trusting girls with wings and magic wands and all too much time to worry about the goings-on of other fairies and meddle in the affairs of people.

Oona, this Oona, is silent. Not just in her speech, but in her steps as we move through the trees, through winter at one step and summer at another. Her walking makes no more noise in snow than it does on fallen leaves.

Her skin is slowly changing its colors, matching our

surroundings. If I look away, try to take in some of the things around us, things I will never have the chance to see again unless events go terribly wrong, she continues to walk. I follow closely. She will not lose me so easily when I am on my way to return victorious.

We walk for at least a dozen years. I have enough years to practice walking without a shadow in the summers, without a smell in the springs, without a rustle in the autumns, without punching through the loose powder of the snow in the winters. Until we come to the final autumn, the leaves softer, wetter, blacker than in the previous years. Oona slows, finally.

A ring of mushrooms waits. For us. Of course I know it's a fairy ring. I have seen fairies in TV shows and movies that are truth, not only in cartoons. Rip Van Winkle fell asleep in such a ring and did not wake for decades. He probably just got lost and had to walk all his years away, then forgot.

Oona steps inside and begins to change, to become less visible. She is not disappearing, she is simply stepping through a doorway that obscures her passage.

I follow. What else should I do with this silent woman? If she enforces the rules of this world, she is no different than the rules of my usual world. Unseen, too powerful, too quiet, too unpredictable.

One foot through the ring, and I smell the musty earth. It is not the smell of my own place.

This is not the way home, I tell her.

I try to step back, but unseen hands shove me from behind, and I fall completely through the doorway. With my reflexes I recover faster than even Blackie would. Spinning and looking shows me only darkness and slump-shouldered things looming in the shadow. Oona is glowing faintly as the other Oona also did in the darkness before she attacked me. Her posture, the slow depth of her breath tells me she is being patient. Why would she be in a hurry? She has me trapped.

"You are welcome and safe," she promises.

The magic fails to punish her for lying, but perhaps it could not hear her or retribution is slow to reach this place.

I can't see anything, I admit to her. If I am lucky, she cannot see my skin redden in shame.

I will make light, she says. No promises this time. I squeeze my eyes shut so that the light will not blind me if she is tricksy.

An orange glow passes through my goggles, through my eyelids, and does not hurt. I open my eyes. The things that were lurking before have become high-backed chairs, overstuffed and upholstered in fabric the color of the ocean at sunset from beneath the surface when the fish come quickly to my beckoning call.

Maybe she wasn't lying.

I sit. My legs are tired after our years of walking.

#

Give me the crown, Oona tells me.

I shake my head no. Probably I should get out of the chair to be ready in case she attacks me. Probably I am too tired to fight her off anyway. *It's mine. It was a present.*

My vassal had no right to give it to you. You have your own magic and no need for the fairy magic anymore.

Perhaps she is angry about it, but her voice is not angry. There is less threat in it than in Bigman asking for the remote control when I'm watching my shows downstairs.

What does it matter to stand a bit more after all this time if it means I get to keep my gifts? Oona remains seated, but I wander the room. There are no doors that I can see, not even the one I entered through, but the place is crammed with furniture of various types. Overstuffed chairs, three-legged stools too small for anything larger than a mouse, low cushions covered in what I suspect is dog hair, and posts undoubtedly for climbing by cats. I use my claw to mark a few stripes on the posts. *Here was a clawed one.*

I look back to Oona. *What is this place? We are not headed back to where I belong.*

Oona pinches the bridge of her nose but does not scowl the way Bigman usually does after the same motion. *These are my audience chambers,* she tells me.

But there is no audience, only the two of us. After I say it, I look more carefully to see whether I am telling the truth. Perhaps I have overlooked some spies. A few windows show night skies, and I peer out them. The stars are wrong, even without lifting my goggles they are too bright a smear across the sky. In the space movies, this is how the heroes know they are not on Earth, but I already know that. Importantly, I do not see any listeners or watchers in the dark. If they lurk, they do so far away.

I am certain I could find a way out one of the windows if Oona were not watching me, and the low drop to the ground below would be nothing at all. But her eyes track me as I wander through her chambers.

Will you keep me trapped here until I give you my crown? I come within striking distance to watch her eyes when she answers. If she answers wrong, I can have her by the throat in a moment. She might be stronger than the other Oona, who I was able to defeat so easily and became my friend after, but I doubt she is strong enough to resist my full wrath.

She sets her elbows on her legs, hangs her head down. As natural as this position looks when Bigman does it, seeing Oona do it reminds me, as if I needed reminding, that she is not at all a human.

No more than I am.

We wait, we two monsters, both for the other to say something that we want to hear.

Finally, Oona sighs, which I have been expecting since she first pinched her nose, and mumbles *No. But you should give it anyway.*

Why?

If I tell you before you take the crown off, the crown itself will ruin it. This does not sound like a lie, but it does not sound like a Truth, either.

So you'll take me away now?

She doesn't respond in words, but she twists what I did not realize was a knob below one of the windows, pulls the door open, and steps through. I follow before I am trapped here.

Oona is glowing faintly ahead of me, and I follow her through trees that have the wrong number of branches, the wrong texture of bark, but all smell the same. We head straight toward the moon. She says nothing for an hour, but when we see light in the distance, she heads toward it and then inside without inviting me. I am not so foolish as to let her leave me behind.

Through the door, and it shuts behind me. Even knowing where it ought to be, I cannot see the knob. Fairy magic is beginning to bore me.

Oona sits in a chair that looks just like her previous seat. I check the room, and when I see my claw marks on the cat posts, I know she cannot be trusted. She has me trapped, whatever she says.

Give me the crown, she says again. A demand, no matter how pleasantly she speaks it.

If Oona asks me for it back, I will return it, but it is not yours and has never been yours.

She says something cruel, and before I can react, she has left through one of the hidden doorways of this prison.

The world below kept me from sleep, but that has left me exhausted, and I sink into one of the soft chairs. I will sleep for only a moment. Just until she gets back.

Chapter Fourteen

I hope I was asleep for only minutes. It would break my heart to find that I have been asleep for thousands of years, that empires have risen and fallen while I slept. That Bigman has finally died of old age while I slept, and denied me my vengeful homecoming.

Oona is staring at me as I gather my thoughts. If Oona has been watching me for millennia, she has more patience than I do.

Is the crown mine to decide about? If it is not mine, if my friend misled me when she handed it over, then we will have words with our hands and our feet and see that I am still stronger. But I hope she did not trick me.

It is yours, this Oona confirms.

Can I leave with it? Can I return home with it?

She doesn't blink. Maybe I have asked this question before and forgotten asking. *I am not stopping you.*

This is not the same as saying yes. When Bigman had my scales, when he had my memories, perhaps the denial would have fooled me, but I am not fooled anymore. The image of the Magus on my skin is giving me wisdom or confidence, or maybe they are the same thing to one like me.

I pull the crown from my head. It is reluctant to go. Holding it in my hands, I spin it. There is no front, no back. A half-twist in the band means there is not even an inside or an outside. I can run my finger around both without lifting it from the surface, and I can push the twisted place around the circlet.

Humans call it a moebius strip, Oona tells me. *It is the embodiment of the sameness between inside and outside.*

Maybe she was only trying to tell me how smart she is, but knowing that the fairies see it this way makes me nearly certain I will make the right decision.

Do you need a reminder? I look to her, even though I am not wearing the crown to know whether she speaks truth. Whether she lies or truths, the fact of answering will provide me certainty.

Sometimes.

I need no reminder that there is no distinction between inside and outside anymore. I trace the edges of the scales where they overlap on my hands, first tracing my left with my right and then my right with my left. *They look like Big, Strong hands, don't they?*

Maybe she doesn't know *The Neverending Story* and the futility of Rockbiter's grasp. I have seen the movie enough times to know it. Enough times that the tape has been nearly burned through and entirely burned into memory.

How long has Bigman kept me trapped? Two years or twenty or a century? However long, his suffering will be shorter when I return. Shorter, but more intense. We will have our reckoning.

Before I can change my mind yet again, my hand reaches out the crown to her. When she takes it, I do not leap for her face and claw out her eyes. My legs barely flex in anticipation, and I sink back into the chair. Either the whole world will have ended when I return, or there is time yet to rest.

Oona bows, Fairy to Dragon. *Wait here.* I oblige.

She steps through the door and before I have even gotten sleepy again, she has returned. In her hands, she holds a small bottle. A potion of some kind, probably. The top is stoppered with a cork, not the kind of top that the perfume buys for his women friends has. I take the bottle when she holds it out.

The liquid inside is thick, and moves reluctantly when I tip the bottle. It fights both light and gravity, moving too slowly and refusing to stabilize to one color but also staying both dark and clear. The cork doesn't move when I try it.

Oona blinks in what I have learned over the centuries of being stuck here is alarm. *Don't open it yet. You will know when.*

What is it? What will happen when I open it?

A life will be lost.

Poison?

She shrugs. *That's an ugly word. When Socrates drank, he did not view it as such but did not deny others would think so.*

This Socrates guy sounds like he was easily fooled. Oona hasn't introduced me to her friends, so maybe all of her friends are foolish.

Are we friends? If she says yes, I will know she is lying. Maybe we are enemies, and maybe not, but the number of my friends is a zero formed into a moebius strip. There are no friends inside, no friends outside. Except Mary and Oona and Blackie and a few others. There is only myself and mother who understand what it is to be us, and only I am here holding this bottle.

I slip the bottle into a pocket I wasn't sure I had. Maybe it is only recently grown.

Oona stands, and holds the door for me.

#

I step through, and the door closes after me, and Oona is no longer with me. She has tricked me once again, but we owe each other no debt of honesty. I gave that up with my crown. Probably that is why she needed it so much, even though it was not hers. Or maybe it was hers, in that place.

The road ahead of me is a beach boardwalk, of the sort that has never graced the corrupted strand near the lighthouse. Boardwalks are not built for the people who live along the beach, nor for the monsters who live with them. Nevertheless, I've seen enough of this kind of show that I know all roads will lead home.

After ten minutes of walk, the sun has fallen ten minutes toward night. I'm still trapped, as always, but not in the lower place.

After twenty minutes, someone is calling me from the beach. A voice I hear sometimes in my nightmares, but not for many years in my daytime. When you can't see very far, you get good at recognizing voices. Annea's father. I've never known his name, and I'm sure he's never known mine. He has been calling for Annea, but he must know that name will lure me also. I have let the falling sun lie to me about being back in my own world.

This is not my world, but perhaps it could be. Isn't it my choice which world will be mine?

I start to run, and the clothes moving against my skin match clothes that Annea used to wear.

See me with love, I tell the world around me. My power has grown enough that maybe I can fool the world in new ways.

"My child!" he promises with joy, and sees me. I run to him, and his arms scoop me into the air. I have flown through Sky and Sea, and they are sad imitators. This feeling, of being accepted for all that I am, this is why Night created Moon and why Moon created Sea. Bigman has kept me small and weak by refusing me this acceptance.

The man strokes my hair, which has grown to be long and beautiful, like Annea's was. He was calling for her. She must be here, too. And maybe the young prince, undrowned. This must be Oona's gift for trusting her enough to give back my crown.

He puts me down and I run to the water, which will always be my first home and must span all possible worlds.

Time passing means not only that the sun has sunk lower to the horizon, illuminating the water in front of me and casting my shadow onto the waves, but that I am hungry.

I dive deep into the water and sing out to the fish. *Come close, and let us be friends.*

None respond, and my eyes cannot see well with my goggles, so I take them off. Still none come, and I can see no better beneath the water.

Come out, come play, little fishies!

I swim and call out to them, and finally there is movement, something coming toward me.

We have never been friends, the kraken and I, but we have been honest with each other.

Come closer, and I'll bite you, girl. Suckered arms punctuate the threat.

I'll show you "girl," I tell him. I reach my hands with their soft fingers, my arms with their smooth, tanned skin, to grab the monster.

Pain, when the kraken's arms grab mine. Pain, when they let go and leave me with pale round welts that remind me of skin that was riven by loss. I can't remember what TV show that was from.

I gasp from how it hurts, and salty water gets into my

mouth and starts me choking. I thrash to the surface and start coughing.

Arms, human arms, are grabbing me, pulling me from the water, setting me down on the beach.

"Annea," he says. Dad says. "Are you okay? I was so worried."

Where is he? I ask. My brother. He should be here.

"Stay calm, I need to get your brother, and then we'll go home and get warm."

While he is gone down the beach, where I can see a small figure in the shallows, I put my swim goggles into a pocket, next to a little bottle I must have picked up somewhere.

The sand is cool and gritty between my fingers, and it gets beneath my nails, but I don't mind.

A lizard hisses at me, tries to bite me, but its teeth are too small to break the skin. Its bite feels like nothing compared to the sting the octopus gave me.

Dad calls out to me, waves at me from where he stands with my brother.

"Let's go home, Annea."

#

Dad is angry again. He's never liked the "little mute" from next door, and he's been especially cruel lately. Mr. Bigman says he is the child's guardian, but dad says that the man can't even take care of a house, so how would he care for a *normal* child, much less… "that"?

I haven't told any of the others at school about my

neighbor. It had been hard enough to make any school friends when we'd moved to Florida, and they definitely wouldn't have understood my friendship with the kid from next door. Mr. Bigman said their name was Lucy, but when I used that name, they shook their head no at me. Mr. Bigman said sometimes they wanted to be called Luke, but they shook their head no at me again.

"What's their name, really?" I asked him.

He pulled on his beard. "Whatever you think it is, it's not."

And they smiled and nodded when he said that, so I've called them Not when names have mattered, which isn't often. We haven't needed words to be friends. Usually, it's pretty easy to figure out what they want, or at least whether they want to play with me in my room or go swimming or watch TV together.

The weather is nice, and the afternoon rains have left the beach smooth. Darren wants to go swimming, which is something Not never turns down. When we first started swimming together, a couple years ago now, I was worried that Not's strange swimsuits would be a problem. I certainly can't swim well enough to be weighed down by the bloom and swell of Not's suit in the water, but Not swims better than both me and Darren.

Dad doesn't like me to take Darren swimming because, honestly, he's not that great a swimmer. The swim coach at school calls him "enthusiastically bad," but the ocean is calm today. It's not the glass flat of the lakes where I spent last summer with my cousins, but it's as close as the Atlantic ever gets to being so.

When they see that we're going swimming, Not runs down the beach and leaps without hesitation into the shallow water. It is only a few minutes before they are beyond sight. The first few times we went swimming, even after Mr. Bigman had assured me that it was safe, it had been alarming how long Not liked to stay under the water and how deep into the waves they liked to swim. I'm used to it now. It's nice to see Not so happy. Dad is angry again because Mr. Bigman has stopped caring for his plants, and they've started dying. To make it even worse, it's attracted a lot of different bugs, and Mr. Bigman keeps feeding the feral cats. That's just made it so there's more of them.

Darren is safe where he's at. The water comes up to only his ankles, and he is squishing his toes into the sand, burying his feet a few inches before pulling them up in clumps of wet sand. Then he washes his feet carefully in the water and starts again.

I spot Not a ways out, but not so far that I can't catch them with the tide this low. I'm able to run halfway there before the water is deep enough that I have to swim. Not waves happily when they see me headed their way, and I show off my crawl stroke, which I've been practicing for weeks. When I'm almost to them, Not takes off again, and it's clear that we are racing. It almost hurts my eyes to watch Not swim. There's no way those strokes ought to produce the movement that they do. Some days, it feels like the ocean itself is colluding with Not to make them faster.

For ten minutes, I crawl after Not, who is swimming away from the afternoon sun. No matter how perfectly I perform the stroke, I can't close the distance between the two of us, and I give up with a laugh when the muscles of my arms signal that they'll start burning if I don't slow down. I'd rather not need to breast stroke the whole way back to the shallower water.

"I've got to go back," I yell to Not, and they nod. It's clear they'll follow me to the shore. We've played these games a lot, and it's hardly even strange anymore that Not doesn't speak.

I start swimming, and I hear Not trailing me. They're always a little reluctant to leave the water. I guess I would be, too, if it loved me the way it seems to love Not.

When I had asked Mr. Bigman if they went to school, he had said "No," but not talked about it since then. It's a shame, really. Our swim coach would die to have a prodigy like Not.

#

Nobody at school understands what it means that Darren died that day. It's hard to tell whether Not understands what it means to drown. Dad's forbidden me to go out except for school, but I've seen Not out swimming in the waves every day, as if they're searching for Darren. He's not coming back. He's dead, and we buried an empty coffin.

Am I horrible for missing Not more than I miss Darren? There's something special about them. I feel connected in a way I don't feel with any other person. Not Darren, not dad, not even my memories of mom.

#

I caught Dad on the phone, yelling at Mr. Bigman about Darren. He said he was going to sue, that it was the fault of "that little monster," and that Mr. Bigman is responsible as their guardian. But Dad is the one who was here, too tired to go swimming with us. He's told me it was my fault for not keeping a better eye on Darren, that Darren was my brother, and it was my duty to care for him. More and more, that doesn't feel true. I know he was supposed to be my brother, but that word doesn't carry any weight in my heart. Barely more weight than "father" does.

We had a fight about it. He tells me I've been acting strange lately. As though my brother dying weren't enough to explain it. I feel like that happened to someone else. I am not the girl who was there when he drowned. My father is the one who was also not there when Darren drowned. Between the two of us, I know who is more to blame. There was a lot of screaming, and I said things I'll probably regret later. Things like "I'm sorry," and "It was my fault." As much as Dad agreed with my words, it didn't seem like his heart was in it.

He is not the one lying awake in the middle of the night, listening in the hope that Darren was just lost, that he washed up somewhere else, that he is home now. I can hear someone in Dad's room, bumping into things that crash to the floor. Dad knows his way staggering and in the dark, and I doubt that it's him. But we have nothing to rob anymore. The magic left when Mom died, and the things started going after as Dad sold them off a few at a time to pay for his sadness. Every once in a while, he'd take us to Disney, as though that could make up for us living in this awful place with the mean kids at school and none of my real friends. I have only one friend, who says nothing. It seems fitting.

I go to see what's happening, which breaks every rule of the horror movies Not wants me to watch with them. They're too young to watch them, surely, but they take such pleasure in things that frighten and disgust me to see on screen. I should stay quiet in my bed, or flee next door, but something makes me go and look.

The door opens silently. A winged figure in white is sitting on top of Dad, pounding at him. There is a glint of metal.

"Monster," I scream, and the angel, which I see now is Not, flees out the window.

I remember this. This is not how it happened, which is why I screamed out monster. I am the monster in this story. Me standing here and me fleeing out the window.

Oona tricked me. It was never the mirror that kept me from seeing myself in it, never my eyes, never my goggles. How many months have I been thinking I was Annea?

I am Knot. The monstrous thief who would take Annea's life in place of my own.

I had thought maybe it would be easier to be her. To be a girl, to be beautiful, to be loved, to be tragic.

And it would have been, probably, but the spell is broken again.

This life isn't mine. There must be some way to give it back, now that I know. I cannot give her back her brother. I cannot give her back her father. But I can give Annea back herself. Maybe.

How do you give back a life you stole without meaning to?

#

Even knowing what I know, that I am not this girl whose body I am stuck inside, that I am instead Dragon, a great and terrible beast, does not let me know how to escape. It is Oona who did this to me, and so I must find her and make her take it back.

With Dad, Annea's dad, I mean, dead, it will only be a matter of time before they come to take me away, back to Annea's family wherever she left them. I still have vague plastic memories of cousins and grandparents and other smiling faces. Of a dead mother, a dead brother, and now a dead father. Loss feels different as a human. It's distracting, and it makes me want to scream and cry to push it away.

I am too busy for such things. I didn't know you could be eaten by another person's memories.

I must find the fairy queen before Annea's grief swallows me whole.

Chapter Fifteen

Annea's body is tall, gangly, uncooperative. I walk it to the place where I met Oona before, and the nose keeps sending me too few smells and the eyes keep sending me too many sights, but none the right one. When I find the shelter, I step inside and close the door, and wait.

Oona is not appearing. Not the Oona who could have chosen to be my friend and not the Oona who tried to be my queen. But someone is breathing heavily, sounding a little panicked. I hold my breath to locate the source of them better and the breather stops making noise. They think they're trickier than me.

When I can't hold my breath anymore, I let it out forcefully. The fairy hiding from me does the same, at the same moment. Annea's thoughts are intruding on mine, and I worry she'll take over again if I don't find Oona soon.

Of course, it's probably just my own breathing.

Annea's brain doubts my magic. *It's not my own breathing. Be patient, girl.*

These legs are too long for this space, and these lungs

are starting to gasp at the stuffy air, and these eyes are starting to cry. She loved me. She did, despite how frail her body is now. How frail it must have been then. It is no use to fight against her body to make it a dragon any more than I could have fought mine to make it a boy or a girl. I open the door, which fails to be magically locked.

I run to the opening to the Cat Kingdom, but it is only a hole in the ground that smells like feral cats and is missing all of its welcome. The queendoms of Fairy and Cat are being denied to me now. Denied to this body, at the least.

I run to the beach. I will swim to Bird, who will not hide themselves from me. Who will have to answer to the peacocks even if not to me.

Annea's body will not swim. It is frightened still of the waves. It is frightened of me inside it, but this is not my choice!

I run back to Oona's lair in case she has returned, thinking she had fooled me into going away.

Oona took myself from me, my crown from me, my crown that would have kept me from being fooled by the illusions of childhood. And what did I get in return for it?

What did you get in return for it?

A potion. I got a potion.

I'm not thirsty, but I drink.

I'm not dizzy, but I fall.

I'm not ready, but I die.

#

I didn't expect death to be such a familiar place, but here I am back in the cat alley.

The birds fly by, trying to taunt me into chasing them. They are no kin of Bird. They are beaked, but their beaks cannot gouge. They are clawed but their claws cannot rake. They tell me they are elusive prey, but even without a crown I know they are liars.

The last time I was here, I was chasing the older Oona, headed to retrieve my scale. This time, I am just being dead. The scale I was chasing is forever beyond my reach, but I still have the copy of Bigman on my arm.

I poke him with a claw. He scowls but doesn't reply. I poke at him again, harder. He dodges.

The rage is trying to rise in me, but I cannot summon the ocean, cannot feel it moving through my veins. Even now, when I am dead and he is a mere discoloration, Bigman continues to treat me as the weaker of us.

I stab at him, hard, and my claw dives deeply into my wrist, nearly skewering his chest.

Tell me how to make this stop, I demand. Why had I thought Oona would be speaking truthfully when she told me the potion would mean giving up a life? Here I am, dead but still stuck. I know the people will be ahead, will demand once more that I choose between boy and girl, between woman and man. Even dead, I am neither. Did the boy stay a boy when he drowned? Did he come here to the cat alley and choose to remain a boy forever?

Bigman says nothing. Merely shrugs and wobbles dangerously toward one side of the edge of his patch of skin, crowded by my claw. I pull my claw out. The hole goes entirely through, but there is no blood to lick away.

Where is my blood?

I stab my other wrist, inside to outside, and still no blood flows. I pierce both of my feet, and stomp bloodlessly in a circle.

You don't have any blood. You're dead.

It is no wonder that mother feels more ancient than the TV says life has been on Earth, because I walk for what must be a million years, pacing near enough the far end of the alley to see the people impatiently waiting to demand I make impossible choices and the endless treadmill of the near end, where no matter how long I walk it is always the same distance to the people.

You're going to wear out your feet of clay, Bigman taunts from my skin. It was a mistake to bring him.

I am much more patient than Mother, but no dragon's patience is infinite.

Not because Bigman said so, and not because I'm bored — I could do this forever without boredom — I don't stop myself from reaching the people at the end of the alley.

I'm a man, says the bearded one.

I know that, I snap back. *I remember. I'm dead. What do I do this time?*

Go this way if you're a boy or a man, he says, and points.

"I'm still Knot," I promise him.

Knot entirely, says the other one. She's been telling me she's a woman, but I don't care. I know her claims already. *You have something inside you that doesn't belong. You are only mostly clay. There is still a pebble at the center that doesn't belong.*

Without blood and other ocean in my body, it's harder to feel what's going on inside, much less control it, but focusing lets me feel that she's right. Something is inside me that doesn't belong.

After I try for probably a couple of years to cough it up, I use my claws to dig carefully into my side. It's not even as messy as swallowing a fish can be. There is discomfort, but no pain. Finally, I have grasped the thing and pull it out, smoothing the edges of the wound as I go until there is only a large dent in my flesh, a hint of the bloodless wound.

It is the stone that the Cat Queen gave to me. I show it to the woman. The man pushes her aside to look more closely.

Oh no, they say together.

You have to choose, he says to me. *Me or her. Who do you want to be?*

Neither, I tell them again.

They put their heads together for a discussion I can't hear and don't care about. I've been here a million years. I can wait a few more minutes.

You can't be neither, but you can be both, the man finally tells me.

Okay, I lie to him.

They both put their hands over the stone where it is sitting in my hand. It starts to bleed, and the blood runs into the holes I made earlier in my hands and feet, and the blood runs into the hole I made earlier in my side.

At first, it is bitter, the smell of cats but made into blood. As more and more is absorbed, I can feel the ocean in me. It hurts, to be remade. I hadn't realized until now just how much I'll owe the Cat Queen for giving me a lifetime.

The pain overwhelms me, and despite the bright sun my vision dims, and when I fall both of the people stop touching me, wipe the blood on their clothes, and return to their affairs.

#

Lizard's feet have been pittering pattering across my clothes, this rag that has never been in my closet and is not any kind of costume, for probably an hour now, and I have only just figured out that I am awake again, lying amid mushrooms and dead roots.

You stink of fur and laziness, the lizard complains. I sit up, and it scurries to the ground, waits in front of me in startlement.

Why are you here? In the dim light, I see that I am in Oona's place again, but the lizard and I are alone.

You would have been trapped by the rock. The feathered one had no strength to move it. The black furred one tried to eat me and would not listen. It took me three days of digging, but I am here to rescue you.

260

Lizards don't have as much facial expression in real life as in cartoons and movies, but the smell of worry lingers in the air, mingling with rising relief. Maybe someday, there will be movies with smells, but not yet.

I'm alive, then. I'm alive, again.

"I owe you," I promise the lizard. It blinks at me.

This place is too cool. It makes me tired, and I need to find a sunny place to warm myself. It runs away, and I am left alone.

I didn't know it would be so exhausting to rise from the dead. Looking out the door, I see a small rock nearby, nothing that I could not have pushed aside myself. The sun is screaming hot violence at me, and I do not have my goggles, and my costume seems like a bedsheet in the light. Better to wait here until the sun sets or the afternoon rains arrive.

The door doesn't object to me swinging it closed to give myself some cool dark while the time passes.

Ahh, little Dragon. I see you have earned the title you claimed without right when we first met.

My eyes had sneaked themselves closed without me giving them permission, but I open them again.

Oona, I acknowledge. *You seem better.*

She does. Even now, she does not have a crown. Her queen must not have returned it. But she is not leaking light, and her dress is mended well enough I can't see the needlework.

What happened to the crown? She points at my unadorned

head. As though I don't know where a crown belongs.

Your queen took it.

Oona does something that makes her dress shimmer, then starts moving toward me.

I don't want to fight, I tell her.

Oh, you've outgrown the need for pain to teach you truth. It will still do so in the future, you know. For now, remember that you agreed to owe me.

If I forgot, it is only because I thought that the debt could be paid to any of her sisters. Giving back the crown was supposed to pay the mortgage. Bigman told me that's what it's called when you shouldn't owe someone but they can claim you do.

Oona comes close enough to touch, and I do not strike her because she doesn't seem to be trying to hurt me this time.

She puts a finger carefully into the holes I've dug into myself in the cat alley. They neither hurt nor bleed, as though they were meant to be there all along.

You've been keeping interesting company. They've taught you some of the blood magic. I thought you would stick to water this time.

She's wrong about everything. The company I kept was boring and trapped me for maybe a billion gazillion years that I could have been watching shows at home with Bigman, if only he hadn't tried to control what I do. Blood magic was Bigman's work. I never used it. Not my fault that blood and the sea are so close to one another.

What do you want? I demand it of her. *Tell me now how I can repay you, or tell me that I never need to.*

Oona laughs. I want to hear it as cruelty, because one need not repay one's enemies except in vengeance, but the laugh is neither cruel nor kind. Being trapped in the cat alley and in the under for so long taught me laughter has more than two colors.

The little girl, Oona says. *We want her. She will become a fairy queen one day.*

I would rather kill you than help you hurt her. I rise to my feet, though I am still tired enough that it would be a burden to have Bigman bring me fried fish if he weren't going to feed it to me one bite at a time. How many years ago did he do so? How many years ago did I forget his sometimes kindness?

Hurt her? Oona's face shows she is shocked. *You can repay my debt with your promise that you will never see the girl again. You would break her, you know. The way you broke the other one. She was also supposed to be a queen, and you ruined her.*

Liar!

"I speak truth," she promises.

When a dragon is upset, it can spark a storm on the other side of the world. China has done nothing to me, and I am sorry for the troubles they will have soon. My control of things far away is weak, so weak.

I will never see the girl again, I say.

Promise it, Oona demands. *Promise you're not lying.*

"I'm Knot," I promise, and Oona doesn't know enough to hear my name.

Chapter Sixteen

My anger wants me to go see Mary right now, just to show that the fairies don't control me. My feet and my hearts have other ideas. They keep steering me toward the lighthouse. Toward the nail. Toward home.

I ignore both and head to the beach, then south toward where Bird must await me.

Bird's mobile dinners do not scream at me this time. They know I've changed and might be hungry enough to eat them without warning.

The door opens at my hand, and Bird is waiting for me in their chair.

I sit in mine, and they serve their terrible tea.

What do I do now? If anyone will know, it is Bird.

Go home, Bird suggests.

I will go home, but I cannot stay. Can I find Annea?

Bird sucks in breath, which makes the sound of a starling. What kind of bird was Bird before they made their challenge? It doesn't matter right now.

There is one who might know, Bird says. *But finding her will be tricky for you.*

They grab my hand and pull my arm full onto the table and exam my new scale. As though they don't remember. When they poke at my wounds, it is too much, and I pull away.

Tell me how I find her, I beg.

Her Tiger will lead you there if you are patient. Go home. Head north.

I leave Bird and walk back along the beach.

#

The lighthouse stands before me, and though it ought to, it does not tremble at my return.

The front door is locked, and this costume I'm wearing makes climbing hard, so I drop my cloth and scale the tower, open my bedroom window, climb inside.

Bigman has left everything as it was before. He must have been dusting in here, too, because it's not any dustier than it was the last time I left. Certainly not the years that would show themselves otherwise.

Naked has never been a costume that Bigman wanted to see me in, so I look through my closet to choose something less likely to make him refuse to talk. He owes me, but he's never admitted that and I don't expect he will now. I find a knight's costume. No armor, no sword, but it is still in its plastic wrapping. He must have ordered this when I asked, then not told me about it. The tunic fits perfectly.

The way I did once before, when my feet were wet and

266

did not have holes in them, I sneak downstairs to his library.

You don't see me, I tell him. But it's an accusation, not a command, and he does see me this time.

He grabs for me, but I dodge. Maybe I'm older than him by now after all the millions of years I spent being dead, but I'm still quicker. He should know from that boring movie that he likes that being quick and being dead go together.

"Where have you been?" He speaks in the language of promise, hope in his voice, but it's unwise to promise things before you know.

I show him how I've made him part of my skin. He grabs me by each hand and sucks his breath in at seeing the holes. I'm starting to regret making them if this is how everyone is going to react. I'll need to choose costumes that have long gloves. Worse, I'll need to wear shoes. He tries knocking me off balance by grabbing my feet, but I make him dodge my claws instead.

I put enough distance between us that he will have to lunge to reach me.

Bigman looks at me wearily. *How was being dead?*

Worse than I expected, I tell him. No reason to lie. He's old and will find out himself soon enough.

Want to go fishing?

I nod, and he goes to his room to change to outside clothes, and I wait for him by the door.

He takes forever, but I don't mind.

Finally, when the sun is almost down, we walk toward

the beach.

Did we ever have a choice to be different? I don't think he knows the answer, but I know I need to ask the question.

"I love you, you know," he promises me.

Why were you so mean to me, then?

He's stopped moving while he thinks. He slumps to the ground, and the lizard comes to lick him, and Blackie comes, sits on his chest purring.

It is the work of only moments to go back to the lighthouse, to the kitchen, and bring him his chalice with some water, some crackers from the cupboard. He drinks and eats without comment. He strokes the holes in my hands and feet when I reach to take the cup from him.

I had no idea. All this time.

No idea what? I demand.

I wait what must be a million years for his response, until the sun has gone down and come back up and I am starving.

Bigman says nothing. Not even when the trees start sprouting leaves for the first time in a decade. Not even when flowers grow through his beard, their roots entangled in the ripening bulb of his heart.

I leave him where he fell and go down to the ocean to catch some fish. Looking back at our tower, light shines from my window. May it guide all who would break upon the shore.